THE ISLAND ARTIFACT

Published in Canada by Engen Books, St. John's, NL.

ISBN-13: 978-1-989473-69-6

Distributed by:
Engen Books
www.engenbooks.com
submissions@engenbooks.com

First mass market paperback printing: September 2020

Cover Design: Ashley Amber Boone

Slipstreamers Committee:
Amanda Labonté
Ali House
AJ Ryan
Ellen Curtis
Erin Vance
Lauralana Dunne
Matthew LeDrew

THE ISLAND ARTIFACT

ALI HOUSE & JD RYOT

ENGEN
BOOKS

CHAPTER ONE

The wind whipped around Cassidy, blowing loose strands of her strawberry-blond hair across her face. As she neared the edge of the cliff, the wind grew stronger, almost threatening to blow her over the edge. Glancing back at the tiny town behind her, Cassidy couldn't believe where she was or what she was about to do. A month ago she would have never thought that travelling to different worlds was possible, but here she was, on the Northern coast of Newfoundland, Canada, about to locate a portal and travel through it to another world.

She still didn't quite understand how it all worked, but it wasn't her job to understand. It was her job to go to these strange lands and bring back anything that might prove useful or interesting. For many years she'd travelled all over the globe searching for long-lost relics, but nothing could compare to the thrill of experiencing a world that other people didn't know existed. Her last trip had been full of drama and danger, but she'd been in tough scrapes before, and this time she was a lot wiser.

To get to the portal, she'd flown into St. Anthony, rented a car, and driven from there to the small town of

Straitsview. The drive had taken about half an hour and through it all she'd kept a careful eye out for the many large moose that roamed the areas. The rental clerk had given her a warning to watch out for them because they could take a car down without blinking (her exact words), and when Cassidy saw her first one, broad and hulking and similar in density to a brick wall, she'd had to admit to herself that it'd be best to keep an eye out and stay a safe distance.

When she reached Straitsview, it was even smaller than she'd expected. The town was basically a handful of roads coming off a stretch of highway, all clustered around a small cove and cliff, wrapping around them like a hug. There wasn't much development up on the cliff, leaving lots of room for walking paths and forested area, which was convenient because it was the path she'd have to take. The area was peaceful and the scenery beautiful, but she wasn't here for that.

She was here for adventure.

First she double-checked the coordinates that Professor Gamgee had given her. He had no idea what was behind most of these portals, so for her second trip through they had decided to just throw a dart at the map and go wherever it landed. A strange thrill ran through her. What kind of world was waiting for her on the other side?

Approaching the cliff, she walked until the tips of her brown hiking boots came to the edge. Looking down, she saw a small landing about ten feet below, jutting out from the rocky cliff face. It was about two feet wide and almost ten feet long. The portal was supposed to be on that landing, which meant that she needed to get down there somehow. Gamgee had provided her with satellite images of the cliffside and the rocks had looked climbable. With the kind of weather this area experienced, anything not sturdy surely would have been blown away ages ago. Pushing her foot into the ground, she checked to see if it was sturdy enough to put in a pin and thread a safety line, but the grass was still damp from the morning dew and she suspected that the pin wouldn't hold. Better to climb down without a line rather than to risk having it break free at an inopportune time. The ledge looked wide enough to catch her if she fell, but there was the chance that she might tumble over the edge and down into the cold ocean waters below. And boy did that water look *cold*.

A large smile broke out over her freckled face, as she stared at the dangerous surf below. Her heart started beating faster, but her palms were completely dry. Cassidy smiled as she took some chalk out of her pocket and rubbed it on her hands. She carefully made her way over the edge and down the side of the cliff. Any other person would have to be crazy to go over an edge like this one, but she lived for this kind of danger. She loved rock climbing, and as soon as she mastered one wall, she immediately set out to find another, more difficult, wall to take on. She loved the feel of fighting against gravity, and the deliberate way that she had to make each move, choosing carefully where to put her hands and feet, making sure that the rocks were secure enough to handle her weight. A couple of times she felt rocks shifting under her weight, but she managed to keep her wits about her and made it to the landing without injury.

When both feet were safely on the ground, she let

out a sigh of satisfaction. It was time to head into the un-known.

Looking around, she tried to see the portal, but noth-ing was visible. Squinting her eyes, she searched for some kind of odd light or weird shimmer, but everything was perfectly normal. The surf pounded the cliff face below her and the wind whistled past. For a second she felt stu-pid, like she'd been set up as part of an elaborate prank. Any minute now Gamgee would pop out with a camera and laugh at how gullible she was. Shaking her head, she told herself that the portals had to be real. After all, she'd been to another world and had seen wondrous things, and the professor had no reason to lie to her or lead her on. The last portal had seemed invisible, so maybe they all were, which meant that even if she couldn't see it, it was there. Taking a deep breath she stepped forward, walking down the length of the landing.

At some point she expected everything to change, but nothing did. There was no flash or sudden alteration in the weather or an appearance of strange new scenery. The waves still crashed and the wind still whistled. The grass under her feet looked exactly the same. She wondered what the odds were that she'd travelled to a world exactly like her own. It had to be a small one — especially for a world with the exact same weather. Staring back along the ledge, Cassidy wondered if maybe Gamgee had been wrong about the location of the portal. She glanced over the edge of the landing, but there was nothing else, only a drop to the surf below. If the calculations were off and the portal was down there somewhere, there was no guaran-tee that she'd be able to reach it. Perhaps this location was a bust.

Sighing at the disappointment, she put some more chalk on her hands and started the climb up the cliff. Seeking out handholds and footholds, she tried to concentrate on her immediate task and not think about how she could be in Egypt exploring ruins or wandering through Mayan temples in Mexico. What if all of the locations were like this? What if she'd gotten her hopes up for nothing?

In a few minutes she'd reached the top of the cliff and was pulling herself onto the green grass. She lay back on the ground and stared up at the sky. Maybe this trip didn't have to be a bust – maybe she could drive to Lanse aux Meadows and look at the Viking ruins. It wasn't very far from here. Sure, everything there had already been discovered, but it'd be more interesting than hanging out in an airport, waiting for a flight back home.

Sighing, Cassidy pulled herself to her feet and started to head back to her rental car, but she'd barely taken two steps before the sight in front of her froze her in her tracks.

CHAPTER TWO

Her green eyes widened in shock. Before going over the cliff she'd been looking at a small town, but suddenly it was ten times that big. Where there was once a handful of dwellings, now multiple houses and streets stretched throughout the area, extending farther than she could see. The forest was still on her left, but part of the clearing she'd walked through to get to the cliff had been transformed into some kind of public park, opening into the streets.

It wasn't only the size of the town that had changed, it was the design as well. The previous buildings had consisted mostly of houses and shops, the majority of which were single-storied, but none higher than two stories. The colours had been muted, with faded blue and white siding and paint. Shingled roofs came in two colours, black or red, with the red mainly reserved for tourist shops and bed and breakfasts, which used red as an accent colour, probably to stand out from the local buildings. What the area lacked in population, it had made up for by spreading the buildings apart, leaving ample room for large yards and walking areas. But now the buildings were smaller and pushed up against each other, leaving little room for sprawling yards. Where one house might have sat, there were now four or five. Instead of muted colours, the buildings were bright and vibrant with natural wood accents. Some had grass roofs, others had clay, and the style looked less North American and more European— although she couldn't say for sure which country exactly. Most of the buildings had two or three stories, but she could see a four-story rising above the others, like some kind of clock tower.

Turning back to the cliff's edge, Cassidy wondered if she was seeing things. Perhaps her brain was trying to compensate for the disappointment she'd felt on the ledge by creating some kind of elaborate mirage. Maybe this time, when she turned around, she'd see spaceships or the Eiffel Tower.

Staring out at the cold, unchanged waters of the Atlantic Ocean, she told herself that it was okay the portal hadn't worked. There were supposed to be a bunch of portals all over the world, so it was okay that one of them hadn't worked. There was always next time. Taking a deep breath, she slowly turned around.

The larger town was still there. As she took a few steps forward there was no shimmer or change in the scene, so it had to be real. Cassidy held back a laugh. The portal must have worked after all. There was probably a one-in-one-billion chance that the landscape and weather would be the same on either side, and she'd lucked out. As soon as she got home she'd have to purchase a lottery ticket.

Pausing, she took a few minutes to observe her surroundings and get a lay of the land. There were colourful banners hanging from buildings, the kind you'd usually see during a fair or event. People strolled along the streets, enjoying the sunny day, in a normal human-like manner. They wore clothing similar to what she'd see back on her world — jeans, sweaters, jackets, and sneakers. The scene was odd, but strangely familiar.

She hadn't been expecting something so... normal. There were no flying cars or weird clothing or futuristic buildings. If she hadn't seen the smaller village before going over the cliff, she'd never believe that she was in another world. Was there some kind of catch? Were there lizard monsters roaming the city? Did everyone here have strange powers? Were the police outfitted with giant mech suits? Well, there was only one way to find out.

Taking in a deep breath, she headed towards the town. She didn't have a particular destination in mind, but if she followed the crowds, surely she'd find something interesting. Maybe she'd be able to find out what had happened to this town to make it change so much.

Walking through the park, she soon reached a wide cobblestone street that seemed to be pedestrian-only. Either side was filled with shops, all bearing signs in two strange languages that looked English-adjacent, albeit with strange characters. She wondered if these languages were spoken on her world or if they were strange hybrids? Most of the shops had bunting in the windows, making her wonder if today was some kind of holiday or festival. She recalled seeing a large field to the East while she was standing on the cliff. If there was a festival, maybe something would be happening there, like a sport or an event or a parade. If she couldn't find anything interesting, maybe that would be her next direction.

She continued to look at the shops as she passed, trying to figure out what each one was. Some were obvious — pastries in the window meant bakery, signs of food meant eating establishment, and racks of clothing meant clothing store. There were a few buildings she couldn't quite make out what they were — probably boring businesses or residential housing.

Groups of people passed her by, laughing and talking excitedly. Everyone seemed to be in high spirits, clapping each other on the backs and saying strange words that she didn't understand. The fashion around here seemed to be thick woollen sweaters, jeans, and boots, and with her hiking boots, jeans, and brown jacket she fit in rather well, and started to walk with a bit more confidence. Eventually she reached the end of the pedestrian street, which was a crossroads. It seemed like a good idea to head towards the field, but what if there was a museum or information centre down one of the other streets. She stared down each path, trying to see if anything of interest might be located down there.

As she turned to her left, she saw a tall blond man wearing a dark blue wool sweater with white accents standing near her. He smiled and spoke, but she couldn't understand a thing he'd said.

Her face twisted in confusion. "Sorry, what did you say?"

Suddenly she realized that she'd spoken. Memories of her first trip through a portal flooded her and she quickly shut her mouth, holding her breath as she waited for this person to react to her strange tongue. Luckily, her fears were for nothing.

The man laughed. "English, yes?" he said, in an accented voice.

She nodded cautiously, carefully watching him.

"Do not worry, most of us speak English. We have a lot of tourists here for the celebration."

"The celebration," she said, relief flooding her. "Sorry, it's my first time here and I forgot to get a map."

"That explains the confused look on your face. The information booth is near the game grounds over there," he pointed east, the same direction where the field should be. "They have maps and schedules and can answer any questions you might have."

She smiled. "Thank you."

"It is not a problem. Happy Landing Day!"

"Happy Landing Day," she echoed back as he walked away. When he was gone, she breathed a sigh of relief. Not only was she in a world that understood English, but some kind of festival was happening today — the kind where there would be lots of tourists. It was going to be even easier to blend in than she'd originally thought. Maybe she should buy two lottery tickets.

An information booth should give her some clue as to what was going on today, and maybe they'd be able to point her in the direction of a museum. Heading towards the field, she passed many jovial faces, and she had to conclude that this festival must be a good one. Judging from the amount of people out and about, most adults were probably excused from work and kids from school, which likely led to the abundance of mirth.

As she neared the field, the smell of pastries and warm spices filled the air. Although she'd eaten earlier in the day, her mouth started to water at the delicious scents, and she had to fight to stay on track. She passed by lines of white booths, all filled with different kinds of sandwiches and pastries and drinks. The signs were in three languages, one of which was English, but the other two were those odd characters. There were booths selling souvenirs and clothing, but she gave them little more than a cursory glance. Although she wasn't here to shop, perhaps she could find something interesting to bring back if nothing else caught her eye.

Finally she spotted the information booth. It was a red and white striped tent, and larger than any of the other booths. It also had a sign with the words 'Information Booth' written in English and about twelve other languages. As Cassidy approached she saw that there were bleachers on either side of the field, where people were sitting and watching. Inside the field were groups of kids playing games like tug-of-war and throwing stones. Her interest was piqued.

Walking into the booth, she saw two women stationed behind a table with lots of paraphernalia on it. One was fair-skinned with short blond hair and was wearing a red sweater with a white cross on it, and the other was brown-skinned with long dark hair, wearing a similar sweater.

"*Hej*," the blonde woman said.

"Hi," Cassidy responded cheerfully. "I'm looking for some information."

The blonde woman nodded. "Here is a schedule for today's activities," she said in an accented voice as she picked up a pamphlet. The cover had the words '*Landing Day Celebrations*' written on it and an image of two groups fighting a tug-of-war battle in the field while onlookers cheered. Cassidy noticed that there were many similar pamphlets on the table, each with different languages on it. She noticed that the one in her hand had a small British Flag in the corner and the words were all in English. Glancing at the others, she recognized a few flags: Denmark, France, and Sweden, but not all of them. Some of them looked like a strange mishmash of flags from her world, while others were completely foreign to her.

"If you're interested in learning more about Landing Day, you can visit the museum on Elmegade," the woman said helpfully, holding out a second pamphlet. "It's free all day today."

Cassidy took the offering. "Thank you."

"You're welcome."

Stepping away from the tent, Cassidy quickly read through the Landing Day pamphlet. It didn't say much about the history of the festival, instead talking about all of the wonderful things a person could experience — like their traditional food and drink, children's activities, adult activities, and evening entertainment. She glanced at her watch, which had been set to the Newfoundland time zone before going through the portal. What time was it here? She looked around for a clock, finding one on top of the tall building that towered over the rest of the town. She smiled as she noticed that it was the same as her watch, 12:10pm. This trip was easy as pie.

The children's games currently taking place would soon be over, and the adult tournament would take place at 1:30pm. She glanced through the tournament activities, sizing them up. There was a tug-of-war, a few strength competitions, and throwing competitions. It sounded interesting. A smile crossed her face as she noticed that anyone could sign up to compete. Originally she'd planned on watching the tournament, but now she was thinking of competing. The events sounded simple enough and she kept in good shape, so why not sign up for it? The pamphlet said that the winners would receive prizes, and while she didn't know what the prizes would be, maybe it would be something she could bring back to Gamgee. It wasn't like she'd be doing something crazy, since anybody could sign up, so why not go for it? Her smile widened as she thought about how exciting it would be to take part in a competition in a strange land. She could be a champion in multiple universes.

Checking the pamphlet again, she noticed that registration would take place between 1:00pm and 1:20pm, so she had plenty of time to kill before then. Her eyes went to the other pamphlet in her hand, the one about the museum. There was a small map on the back with instructions on how to find it, and a few review quotes saying how interesting and detailed the museum was. Shrugging to herself, Cassidy decided that she might as well head over there and try to figure out what exactly this world was all about.

CHAPTER THREE

The museum was smaller than she'd expected. It was on the same pedestrian street she'd entered the town through, but close to the crossroads. The building was a converted two-story house, painted white with red shutters and a red door. There was a quaint feeling about it, as if somewhere inside was a grandmother eager to invite you in for supper. A sign was hung over the door, but it was simply two words (both unknown to her), and other than some kind of 'hours of operation' sign, there was nothing else to give her a clue about the contents within. When Cassidy had first looked at it she'd imagined some kind of quaint tea shop or maybe a private club.

When she walked through the front door she found herself in a small entryway, probably the former front porch, with entryways to the left and right. There was a staircase in front of her, cordoned off with a rope barrier that likely led to the second floor. A desk was to her right and she was quickly greeted by the person sitting behind it, brown-skinned with short dark hair, wearing a white button-up shirt.

"Glædlig Landingsdag," they said cheerfully, smiling

widely.

Cassidy nodded and smiled. There was a word in there that sounded like 'landing,' and since she knew today was something called Landing Day she assumed that this was a greeting she'd hear a lot today.

"Hello," she said, before the person could say anything else, being careful to sound as Anglophone as possible. Cassidy could speak other languages, but these two were something she'd never come across before, and it was a relief that people seemed fluent in English here. She made a mental note to find some pamphlets with these languages to take home and see if they had any resemblance to anything back on her world.

The person at the desk nodded and switched to an accented English, giving Cassidy a brief introduction to the museum, telling her how it had been built hundreds of years ago to house the story of this town and to collect important artifacts back from the first landing in the 10th century. Normally they requested a small fee to view the history, in order to maintain the house, but on Landing Day entry was free and all were welcome. Once the spiel was over, the person also recommended that Cassidy start with the door on the right.

Cassidy thanked them for the information and walked past the desk, heading into the room to the right. It was a large room, probably a former living room or dining room. There was an introductory plaque with information in three languages, which she soon learned were Danish, Beothuk, and English. The first two were the official languages of the island, and the last was the most common tourist language. As Cassidy continued to read she learned that the town she was in was called Vandby, and that it was on the island of Vinland, which was a region of Denmark. The town had been built close to the original landing site of the Vikings, yet far enough away that they could preserve what remained of the site.

Pausing to recall what she could of Viking history back in her world, she figured that the splitting point for the timelines seemed to be when the Vikings first landed on this island. In this world it seemed that the Vikings and the indigenous peoples got along rather well and were able to co-exist in harmony with each other. As time passed, more Vikings settled here, building towns along the vast coastline, and eventually they began to intermingle with the indigenous peoples. Cassidy couldn't help smiling as she wondered what it must have been like for the British when they 'discovered' this island hundreds of years later, only to find out Vikings had already settled here.

Moving through the museum, she read about how this island was shaped and changed by this harmony between the two peoples, and how it eventually came to join the country of Denmark. Cassidy felt an itch to get her hands on a history book to see how the rest of the world had changed because of this. Were there countries that no longer existed? Had new countries been formed? What kind of ripple effects had this one change created? Or were there other changes from earlier that had led to this?

She paused to think about all the ways the world would be different if only 'B' had happened instead of 'A.' The possibilities were endless. Perhaps that was why there were so many portals — they all led to worlds where the paths had diverged and changed.

Focusing back on the world she was in, she looked over all the artifacts, which were mainly personal effects and tools. There were maps and drawings to help add a visual element to the history and timeline. Eventually she made it to the final room. There were more pictures along the walls, but in the middle of the room was a pillar holding a statue in a glass box. The pillar was encircled by a rope barrier, which she found strange, since nothing else had been barred off, other than the staircase. She immediately drew closer to the glass box, curious.

The statue inside consisted of two pieces of wood, one light brown and the other red, intertwined in an intricate way. It seemed to be made of four pieces of wood, two of each kind, that spiralled upward and around each other. The piece was about four inches in diameter at the bottom and eight inches high. About halfway up, one side started to slant inward while the other remained straight, and when it reached the top the spiral became thick and flat. The top then curved downward, creating a kind of loop, thinning out even more as it reached the bottom, where the small strands created a braid that encircled the base. The ends of the braid seemed to disappear into the base, creating the illusion that this was all one piece. Cassidy couldn't imagine anyone carving something so intricate and wondered if the wood had somehow been designed to grow that way.

Moving over to the display on the wall, she read about how this statue was hundreds of years old and was one of three that had been created to symbolize the under-standing and respect that existed between the indigenous peoples and the Vikings. It was called Harmony, and the other two, Unity, and Peace, were in other cities on the island. It didn't say anything about how the artifact had been created, but mentioned that the light brown teak wood was from a tree popular in Denmark and the red wood was pine from this island which had been dyed with red ochre, an important pigment to the Beothuk. A few close up pictures showed that there were carvings in the wood — runes carved into the pine and geometric designs carved into the teak. The display gave a loose translation of what the carvings meant, which was some kind of retelling of the first landing from both perspectives.

Even though there were pictures, Cassidy felt the desire to leap over the rope barrier and remove the glass box so that she could get a closer look at the artifact. She'd never do such a thing, as it'd surely end with her being forcibly removed from the building, but her hands itched to get closer. Nothing like this existed on her world. And knowing that it had been created centuries ago made her want to examine it thoroughly.

A thought formed in her mind and she pressed her lips together, suppressing a smile. Perhaps there was a way that she could get a better look at the statue without involving the local authorities. Glancing around the room, she started taking note of the security measure around the museum. There were no cameras that she could see, and she couldn't find any sensors along the walls. The windows seemed to be reinforced and nailed shut, but not barred. If the rest of the museum had the same lax security measures then maybe she could wait until nightfall, sneak in, and get a good look at the artifact on her own terms.

Just the thought of sneaking in after dark and having the place all to herself started to get her heart pumping and she felt a familiar tingle in her fingertips. Perhaps it was the relative safety of this world, but she felt like she could do anything. It wasn't like she'd be around to deal with the consequences, after all.

It would be risky, but she liked risk. And there wasn't much else in this town to get her blood pumping. Sneaking into a museum after dark seemed like just the thing to make this trip more interesting.

CHAPTER FOUR

After finishing up her reconnaissance of the museum's security measures, Cassidy realized that the registration for the tournament had opened up, so she quickly made her way back to the field. It was a great day for an outdoor festival. The air was crisp with a cool breeze, the sun was high in the sky and there were only a few fluffy white clouds floating around. She noticed that a lot more people had gathered around the field, eating and drinking and talking excitedly. Perhaps it was the energy of the crowd or the beautiful weather, but she could feel her excitement rising.

Looking past the Information Booth, she spotted a tent that said 'Sign-Up' in numerous languages and made her way over to it. She wondered what Gamgee would say when she found out that she'd spent part of her time in this world playing games. Then again, he hadn't given her a specific item to find or task to do, so why shouldn't she get to enjoy herself? Considering where this town was located, there wasn't much that she could do. She could see the original landing site, but suspected that it wouldn't be much different from the one back on her world. And there was no point in renting a car and driving all the way to the other side of the island. Not only would it take almost half a day of driving just to get there, but there was no guarantee that she'd find anything more interesting over there than she could find here.

She also felt nervous about straying too far from the portal. If the weather changed it'd be too dangerous to climb down the cliff and she'd be stuck here for however long it took the weather to change back. If she wasn't on her world by midnight, the professor would think that she'd run into trouble, and if she didn't show up for a couple days then the professor would probably think she wasn't coming back. It was much safer to stick around this town and take it all in. If she came back here a second time she'd try exploring further.

Making her way into the the sign-up tent, she joined the line of people wanting to compete. As she waited, her mind drifted towards the museum adventure she'd be having later tonight, but she quickly shook those thoughts away. Now wasn't the time to think about that – now was the time to get into the tournament headspace and prepare for what she was about to do. Even though nobody knew who she was, she didn't want to make a complete fool of herself by failing horribly.

"*Velkommen,*" the person manning the sign-ups greeted her as she arrived at the front. The woman had fair skin, black hair, dark brown eyes, and a wide smile on her face. Cassidy wondered how long the woman had been politely greeting people and if she was getting tired of it yet. Cassidy knew that she'd be exhausted and frowning after twenty minutes, but this woman seemed to have endless cheer. Perhaps that was why she'd been placed here.

"Hello," Cassidy said politely. "I'm here to sign up for the tournament."

"Ah, yes. British?"

Cassidy nodded, figuring that it was safer than taking a chance and mentioning a country that might not exist.

"Your name?"

"Cassidy Cane."

"Your preferred languages?

"English, please." She briefly considered mentioning her other languages, but stopped because of the same reason — they might not exist in this world.

"And is this your first time competing?"

"Yes, it is."

The woman smiled again and nodded. "Once we have all the competitors signed up, we will divide you into groups by size. There will be a light-weight, middle-weight, and heavy-weight division, and each will have a top three rank, who will win prizes. Each division will compete at the same time, but you will be in different areas of the field. If you would like to read about the contests, there's more information over there." She pointed to the side of the booth, where there was a table with small piles of paper on it.

"Thank you," Cassidy said, before wandering over to the table. A few people were milling around nearby, with almost twenty other people inside and around the tent. She briefly wondered which people would end up in her weight class before turning her thoughts back to the contests. After she figured out what each of the competitions involved, then she'd start sizing up the competition.

Picking up one of the papers, she saw that there were five competitions: axe throwing, stone throwing, archery, tug-of-war, and wrestling. They were all based on traditional island games that were played in the past. The descriptions weren't very in-depth, but from what she could make out they seemed similar to the kinds of activities she liked to take part in. As long as the games didn't involved turning into lobsters or using psychic powers, she should do quite well.

After a few more minutes, registration was closed and the volunteers were instructed to gather together. The organizers started calling out the names for each group, usually in a couple different languages. Cassidy had a feeling that she'd be put in with the light-weights since she was a trim 5'3, and sure enough, she was. Five others were sorted into her group, bringing the total to six, while eight people were put in the middle-weight, and eight in the heavy-weight. She exchanged looks with her other competitors, smiling politely but ready to get on with it. Sizing up her competition, she had a feeling that a couple of the others could give her a run for her money, but didn't feel dismayed. She didn't want this to be too easy.

Once the groups were sorted and appointed a volunteer as their leader, they were led through a partition in the back of the tent and onto the field. The smell of freshly cut grass and fairground foods wafted through the air. The groups clustered at the back of the field as the tournament announcer introduced the event in multiple languages while the large crowd gathered in the stands cheered.

Finally, it was time to compete. Cassidy felt a surge

of energy as she made her way over to the archery set-up with the rest of her group, led by Karla, their team leader. Karla's expression was much more serious than the volunteer who'd signed her up, but Cassidy assumed it was warranted, since they'd all be playing around with sharp things soon enough.

The archery rules were fairly simple. They'd be shooting arrows at the target and would get points depending on how close to the centre each arrow fell. They would get one practice arrow, which wouldn't be counted, and which Cassidy was thankful for. These bows were wooden and of a basic design, and the arrowheads looked to be made of carved stone, like they would have been back in Viking times. Neither would be as easy to control as the modern bows and arrows she was more familiar with.

There was no assigned order, so the first person to shoot was the one who volunteered the fastest. If the equipment had been more familiar, Cassidy would have jumped right in, but she held back. She watched how the others handled the bow and arrows, hoping to pick up on a few tips. The target they were shooting at was a large circle with a small red bullseye in the centre, a blue circle around that, then a green circle, then a yellow, and then a white background. The young man who'd volunteered to go first seemed unperturbed by the rudimentary items and confidently took aim, hitting the blue for his practice shot. His next two shots were also in the blue, with the third one getting so close to the red that they had to bring a judge in to confirm that it was actually in the blue. It was obvious that this wasn't his first time competing. Cassidy paid careful attention to the way he held the bow and pulled the string back, and how much tension was in his arms.

She decided to go fourth, figuring that after watching a few more people shoot she'd be as ready as possible. When the wooden bow was placed in her hands, she felt she had a pretty good idea of what to do. Knocking an arrow, she centered it on the bow and pointed it at the target. Pulling the string back, she took in a breath and carefully aimed, pretending that she was back in the temple in Yucatan, trying to set off traps from a safe distance. Her accuracy during that adventure had been perfect, but she'd been using her own equipment.

Her first shot landed in the green, but it was only her practice shot and it was close to the blue. She readjusted, landing the next shot in the blue, much to her delight. Her next shot went in the blue again and her final was in the red, which was extremely satisfying. Nobody else had landed in the red yet, so she had that as a bragging right, even if she messed up everything else.

After the final person in her group finished shooting, they all received a round of applause from the audience. While volunteers in blue shirts took away the arrows, Karla informed the group that they'd be staying here for the axe-throwing. A volunteer brought in a basket of small handaxes as Karla informed them that the rules for this contest would be the same as the last — one practice throw and then the next three would be scored.

Cassidy preferred archery, but she'd thrown a few weapons on occasion, including an axe. Hers had been larger than what they were currently provided with, but she'd also been using hers more to distract and discourage the people chasing her than to actually hit them.

As before, she used her time to watch the other competitors and their technique in holding and throwing the axes, using it to give her an idea of what to do. When her turn came, she did her best, but it took her a while to get used to the weight of the axe and she only managed to get in the green and blue. Luckily her score was on par or better than the others. And she was still the only person in both rounds to have hit the red.

After this contest, Karla led them across the field, where a pile of strange large stones had been gathered. The stones were smooth and oval in shape, with holes in the middle of them, making them look like squashed donuts. Karla picked up one of the stones and demonstrated to the group the correct way to throw it. Standing with her left foot in front of her right and the stone held with her right hand around the shorter end, she swung it down along the right side of her body before bringing it back up. She swung it three times, building up momentum, and on the third time she let go, arcing it across the field. Cassidy had no idea if this was considered a good distance for a throw, but the form was beautiful. While the stone was being retrieved, Karla demonstrated the left-handed throwing style, only without releasing the stone. She let the group know that if they threw the stone any other way, their score would not be counted and they would not get a re-throw. They had two chances to throw, and the field would be cleared after each person's second attempt.

Cassidy went over the throwing technique in her head as she watched the others take their turns. By the time it was her turn to throw, she realized that she hadn't been paying attention to where the stones had landed and had no clue what distance she was trying to beat. All she could do at this point was try her best. And if she was terrible at this round, at least she could think back on her awesome archery skills.

Wiping her hands on her jeans, she picked up a stone, planted her feet, and threw the stone as far as she could. After her second throw, she still had no idea how well she'd done, but at least she hadn't accidentally hit herself in the leg with it or let go of it while it was behind her. One of the throwers after her let go of the stone too soon, and cried out in annoyance as it flew only a few feet before thudding to the ground. Luckily he had a good humour about it, raising his arms in triumph as the crowd chuckled.

Soon the third contest was over and there were only two more to go.

As the group moved on to the next contest, Cassidy noticed that most of them were more focused on winning than being congenial; spending their time psyching themselves up for the task at hand. Two of the group were laughing and chatting with each other, not worried about winning or even scoring highly, but they seemed to be the outliers. Cassidy was just as determined as the former, but she made sure to occasionally smile politely to the other two, just to be nice.

Gathering around the wrestling circle, Karla explained that they wouldn't have to fight everyone else in the group. Instead they would each have two fights, with the people closest to their own apparent size and strength. Staying within the wrestling circle, they were to try and wrestle their opponent to the ground, getting both of their shoulders to touch the ground. If one of them was to step out of the circle twice then they'd both be eliminated, meaning that each of them would have to do their best to stay within the circle. As she looked at the circle, which had been sprayed onto the grass, Cassidy's competitive side quickly rose to the surface, and she had to stop a wide smile from breaking out across her face. Archery and throwing things was fun, but there was something about one-on-one competitions that made winning more satisfactory. Although she hated to lose, she had no problem being bested by someone who was genuinely better than her.

She was on the lower end of the weight class, and the way that the rounds worked out, she would be fighting first and second last. Normally she'd prefer to watch her opponent fight someone else, to get an idea of what their style was like, but she didn't have a choice in this matter.

Standing in the circle, she bent her knees and crouched down to lower her centre of gravity. Her opponent was a young man with roughly the same build as her, and one of the two men who still had a sense of humour about these games. When the whistle blew they both sprang into action, quickly ending up in a grapple. Cassidy turned and threw the man to the side, but there wasn't enough force to send him to the ground, only to break the grapple. She stayed low and waited for him to attack. He rushed forward, preparing to grapple again, but she side-stepped him and used his own momentum to throw him to the ground and quickly pin his shoulders down. After Karla declared her the winner, Cassidy held out a hand to her opponent to help him up, which he took.

"Good fight," he said once he was on his feet, smiling at her.

"Same," she replied, returning the smile.

Two new competitors stepped into the circle, one of which was Cassidy's next opponent. She watched carefully, hoping to glean some information about the woman's fighting style. The match lasted longer than Cassidy's had, but ended with her future opponent winning. The rest of the matches were about the same length, although one barely lasted ten seconds.

When it was time for Cassidy to get back in the circle, she stepped inside and immediately took a low stance. Her opponent was the kind of person who took these games seriously, so she knew that this match wouldn't be as easy as her first one — unless one of them slipped up. Her opponent was a woman who was marginally shorter but more built, and her starting stance was also a low one. When the fight started they rushed into a grapple, but neither seemed to be getting the upper hand. They were both too grounded for the other person to knock to the ground. The grapple broke and they backed up. Cassidy tried to think of a new plan of action, but didn't have much time before her opponent rushed at her. Cassidy tried the same move from before, but her opponent seemed to have been expecting it and tried to reverse it. Cassidy stumbled back, dropping to one knee, but didn't fall. Her opponent came for her, but Cassidy quickly rose, moving to the side and away from the attack.

The match was looking to be one of the longest in their group, with no clue yet as to who would be the winner. After a few more unsuccessful grapples, Cassidy knew that she needed to take a risk if she wanted to win this. The next time they met in a grapple, she dropped low to the ground, throwing her opponent over her. Landing on her side, Cassidy was careful not to accidentally touch both shoulders to the ground. She turned and lunged for her opponent, who had also landed on her side. Grabbing the woman's shoulders and pushing them the ground, Cassidy couldn't help feeling elated. A win was great, but a hard earned win somehow felt even better.

Her opponent looked displeased, but took the hand Cassidy offered and thanked her for the match. Cassidy kept her smile to an appropriately humble size, and thanked her opponent before falling back in line to watch the final match. It was hard for her to concentrate, though, as her mind was trying to tally up where she might be in the standings for her group. As far as she could tell, she was headed for a podium finish, provided on how she performed in the final round.

The last contest was tug-of-war, but it wasn't exactly like she'd ever played before. It would be person against person, with two matches each — against the same two people as the wrestling matches. But instead of standing up, they'd be sitting down, facing each other, with their feet pressed up against a short wooden board that had been topped with foam. The goal was to try and pull the flag that was on the middle of the rope towards yourself, and maybe your opponent as well.

"Let's have a good match, eh?" her first opponent, the man she'd pinned in wrestling, said.

Smiling, she nodded, glad that he would be her first match. It was daunting to go first in a game she'd never played, but her upper body strength was good and that's what she'd mostly be relying on. Sitting on the ground, she placed her feet against the board and grabbed the rope, readying herself.

When the match started, her opponent put up a good fight, apparently being better at tug of war than wrestling. However, he couldn't help losing small increments at a time until, eventually, the flag was over on Cassidy's side.

"Good match?" she asked him as they walked back to their group, breathing heavily.

"Quite good," he replied. "You gave a good fight."

His attitude reminded her of an old friend from university that she used to train with. No matter how often something went wrong, a smile always founds its way on his face. He looked at every failure as an opportunity to learn and refused to let a bad day stop him from achieving his goal. When he won, he was graceful and humble, thanking opponents for a good match, and if he lost, he was just as graceful. The training room always felt better when he was around.

Watching the other matches, Cassidy noticed that most of them were lost by the rope slipping through someone's fingers. Only one match, the one right before her second, was lost when one of the opponents was pulled over the board, landing on their side. It was at that moment Cassidy realized why the foam was on top, so it could help cushion the blow if someone happened to smack into it. Although the person seemed fine, she resolved to try not to let that happen to herself.

Her opponent had a determined look in her eyes as

they took their places, and Cassidy knew that this would be a tough fight. The worst part about competing with someone you'd just bested was that the previous defeat was still fresh in their mind, and they were ten times more determined to beat you. Planting her feet firmly, Cassidy gripped the rope tightly and waited for the inevitable starting whistle.

The first few seconds were a deadlock, the flag hovering over the centre, moving only the slightest either way. Cassidy could feel her muscles straining as she pulled, trying not to lose any ground. She thought of all those hours she'd spent working out and honing her skills so that she could climb cliffs and balance on thin rope bridges, cut her way through jungle vines and dodge traps. There was no way she was going to lose this. The only problem was that her opponent seemed equally as determined.

They both strained against the other's strength, sweat beading on their foreheads. If a person managed to gain a little ground, it wasn't long before the other gained it back. For a second, Cassidy wondered if this match would last forever and if she'd be trapped here in this eternal deadlock for all time. As they continued to pull, Cassidy could feel herself starting to lose ground and not winning it back. Her opponent was strong, and Cassidy could feel her arm and back muscles crying out in pain. If she stood any chance of winning, she'd have to bring something else to the fight. Allowing her knees to buckle slightly, she leaned back, lowering the angle of the rope, before trying to straighten out her legs. Her hope was that the sudden change in the rope's position, paired with the combination of her arm and leg muscles working together, would be enough to win, and it almost was. Her opponent lurched forward, losing precious inches of the rope, but stopping herself from going over the board. She was now trapped in a position where her shoulders were almost past her knees, but still wasn't ready to give up. Cassidy knew that she couldn't risk losing this momentum and she leaned further back, promising her body that once this was over she'd stay away from playing tug-of-war for a long, long time. After a few strained moments, her opponent toppled over, letting go of the rope and sending Cassidy to the ground. Cassidy's muscles cried out in pain and she knew that she'd have to take it easy for the next little while, but then the roar of the crowd filled her ears and she knew that it had been worth it.

Once all the contests were wrapped up, the competitors headed back to the sign-up tent, which had been transformed into a kind of waiting area, complete with water, juice, and pastries. They were told to wait while the judges tallied up the scores and prepared to announce the winners. As Cassidy took a bite of one of the fruit-filled pastries, she came to the conclusion that even if she'd come in dead last, it would be worth competing just for the food. Watching her first opponent take a large bite out of a chocolate concoction, she suddenly understood why he was so jovial despite not doing very well. He had this tournament all figured out.

When the scores were finalized, the competitors were brought out to the field again and greeted with a large cheer from the crowd. The announcer thanked all of the competitors and then announced the winners, starting with the light-weights. Third place went to the woman she'd fought so hard against, and after second went to a man who'd excelled at the last two contests, Cassidy couldn't help feeling her hopes rising. When they called out her name as the first place winner, she felt proud. Taking her place next to the other two, she bowed her head in thanks as she was given a medal and something that looked like a thin, sheathed knife. Looking out over the crowd, she was filled with a warm glow of accomplishment. Not too bad for someone who'd only appeared on this world a few hours ago.

CHAPTER FIVE

After all of the other winners had been declared, the tournament ended and people started wandering away from the field. People Cassidy didn't know congratulated her on her win, and she gave them all a polite smile as she made her way over to a quiet area outside the field where she could examine her prizes in detail. The medal was round and had a large '1' on it, with some words in the native language. Although she doubted that it was made of gold, it looked like it could be gold-plated. Or maybe it was made of some kind of strange material that only existed on this planet.

Moving on to the next prize, she carefully withdrew the knife from the sheath. It was one foot long and quite thin, only about an inch and a half at the thickest part, drawing to a point at the end. Carefully testing the edge, she realized that it was quite dull and was likely intended to be a decoration instead of an actual weapon. The blade wasn't perfect and seemed to be pounded into shape instead of mass-produced, but it had character to it. The sheath had two pieces of leather coming off the side with a loop at the end, one near the tip and one near the handle, and she supposed that it was intended to be worn with the knife parallel to the ground. The handle was wooden with a large, round metal cap on the end. Giving the metal cap a closer look she saw that some kind of strange rock had been set into it. The rock was the size of a quarter, but it had a quartz-like structure to it and was the kind of black that shone in brilliant colours whenever the light hit it. It was mesmerizing.

Holding the knife, she figured that this would be a sufficient enough relic to bring back. She didn't know what Gamgee would do with a dull blade or a strange rock, but he'd probably have some fun trying to figure out what everything was made of. She decided she should also pick up a book or two on the history of this world, so that they could learn more in case they ever wanted to come back. She had a feeling that Gamgee would appreciate something more than her second-hand knowledge from her visit to the museum.

A smile crossed her face — the museum. There was no way she'd leave this world without getting a closer look at the artifact. After all, she was an archeologist and it was her duty to find strange objects and learn whatever she could about them. She'd be doing her profession a disservice by walking away from something so intricate.

Tucking the knife and medal carefully into her backpack, she came up with a game plan. It was late afternoon now and the museum didn't close until 6pm. It would be best for her to wait until dark, when things quieted down in that area of the city, before going ahead with her plan, which left her lots of time to buy a book or two and maybe find a bit of supper. Of course, she'd need some money to pay for those things, and she didn't have any of the local currency on hand. Hopefully this town had a pawn shop close by.

She decided to head back to the information tent, as they'd already proven to be helpful. She didn't want to ask a random stranger, because there was a chance they'd watched her win the competition and she didn't want them to think that she was immediately trying to hock her prizes. She hoped that the people working the information booth had been too busy working to watch the tournament.

Although the games were over for the day, the information booth was still being maintained. Thinking back to the pamphlet she'd read earlier, Cassidy recalled that the day's events would be brought to an end with fireworks after darkness fell. Everyone was invited to gather at the field to watch together, and Cassidy wondered if the other booths would be open that late, selling food and souvenirs. A sudden thought hit her — the fireworks! That would be a great time to break into the museum, when everyone else's attention was towards the sky. She quickly filed that piece of information away for later.

The same person who'd helped her earlier took out a small paper map of the central part of the city and marked a pawn shop, a couple bookstores, and a few restaurants for her. Cassidy thanked her and headed off.

A few minutes later, she found a shop with a large window full of a variety of items. It was mostly giftware, a bit of furniture, and a few musical instruments; some of which looked similar to things on her world. Other items looked like they'd been made by an artist that had been half-awake and blindfolded as someone else described an object. Going through the shop door, she heard a small tinkling sound announce her arrival and was immediately greeted with a musty smell. The man working the counter looked up from what he was doing and nodded at her. She nodded back before moving into the shop, taking in all the strange objects inside. There were a few things that she had no idea what they'd been meant for, but most of the objects looked antique — aka expensive — or not as interesting as the knife she'd won.

Curiosity satisfied, she walked over to the counter. "Hello," she said cheerfully. "English?"

The shopkeeper nodded. He pushed aside something that looked like a word puzzle, with half of the answers filled in. "How may I help you?" he asked, his accent thicker than any other she'd heard today.

"I'm looking to trade." She reached into one of the pockets of her backpack and took out a couple of gold coins that Gamgee had given her. "Do you take gold?" As she put the coins on the counter she hoped that gold existed in this world and that it was still worth a lot of money. If this world had an abundance of it, the value would be terrible. Should she have gone with silver instead?

The shopkeeper picked up one of the coins and examined it. "Well, I cannot give you much," he said. "Although I can tell that these are mostly gold," he squinted and brought the coin closer to his eyes, "seems to be some copper in there. I cannot tell where they come from or if they are of much value, so although I cannot place the country of origin, they look like something a trader might be interested in. Where did they come from?"

Cassidy shrugged. "Sorry, they were a gift from a friend overseas. Well, former friend," she added, hoping that would stop him from asking more questions.

"I can give you this," he counted out some bills and placed them on the table. Cassidy picked them up and counted them, still unsure what the currency was like over here. But it seemed like a good amount, and the shop-keeper seemed honest enough, and she thought it should at least get her some supper.

"Seems fair," she said, and they made the exchange. "Oh, could I ask you a question?" she added.

He frowned but then nodded, so she took that as a yes.

She reached into her backpack again. "I'm not looking to sell this, but could you tell me something about the rock in the handle?" She took out the knife, still in its sheath, and held it towards him.

A slight smile crossed his face. "Ah, an ornamental Viking Seax..." He leaned in closer to look at the handle. "That is a piece of a space rock. Every few years or so a couple fall from the sky. Scientists have studied them a lot, so the rest get used for ornamentation or decoration. Mostly jewelry. It's not worth a lot."

Her mind started racing a million miles an hour. Meteorites fell from the sky every few years? And in such supply that they were no longer something amazing but instead were almost as common as ordinary rocks? What kind of crazy world was this? Did they feel like dinosaurs with all the space rocks falling down? Did dinosaurs exist on this planet millions of years ago? She had so many questions she wanted to ask, but didn't want to push her luck with the shopkeeper's patience.

"That's what I thought," she bluffed, returning the knife to her backpack. "Thank you. Happy Landing Day."

He grunted a goodbye before turning back to his puzzle, and she quickly walked back onto the street.

***

An hour later she was in a pub, planning the museum break-in while she waited for her meal. She'd chosen a pub for dinner because she knew the food would be affordable, but also because it was likely to be loud and crowded enough that nobody would pay her much attention. A few people had recognized her from the tournament and congratulated her as she walked in, but after that she'd mostly been left alone. The pub was styled like an old cottage, with large wooden beams and a few fireplaces. It had a cozy feel to it, with low lighting and well-worn furniture, but it was boisterous enough to keep her on her toes.

After finding a seat near the back and placing her order, she'd set about rummaging through her backpack, looking for items that could be of use during the break-in. There wasn't a lot of room left in there, as she'd ended up purchasing three books instead of the one she'd been planning on buying. After looking at the prices of the books, she realized that the gold coins had fetched her enough to buy more than she'd anticipated. Figuring that it'd be better to be safe than sorry, she purchased an English-language history book and two more books, one in each of the regional languages. Setting the books aside for the moment, she continued taking stock of her supplies.

She quickly found a lockpick, penlight, and camera, and placed them in pockets where they'd be easily accessible.

The server arrived with her meal, interrupting her thoughts, and Cassidy quickly put everything back in her backpack and set it aside. For a second she couldn't remember what she'd ordered, but then saw that it was some kind of cold chicken sandwich with pickled vegetables on a strange kind of bread with a side of fries. She wasn't too sure about it, but it had a star next to it on the menu, signifying that it was one of their most popular dishes.

Eyeing the sandwich thoughtfully, she picked out one of the vegetables and tested it. It was crisp and slightly pickled but also sweet. The flavour reminded her of a banh mi, so she picked up the sandwich and took a bite. It was quite delicious. The spice mix was unfamiliar, but it worked with the cold ingredients.

Finishing the sandwich, she took her time munching on the fries and going over the steps of her plan in her head. During her examination of the museum she'd noticed a back door, which would be the best way to sneak in as there'd be fewer passersby, and she could take her time unlocking the door. The penlight would provide a concentrated beam of light and wouldn't be as obvious as a flashlight, but she'd still have to be careful about where she shone it and would have to use it sparingly. Once she reached the artifact, it'd be best to take it to a different room, where her examination wouldn't be noticed by anyone walking by.

A voice in the back of her head said that if sneaking into the museum was going to be so easy, then it should be just as easy to take the artifact and bring it back to her world. They had two others on the island, after all, so would they really miss this one?

Giving herself a mental shake, she tried to bring her thoughts back to the plan. Normally her modus operandi was to recover lost items, not to steal them. But it wasn't like she could stay here and pretend to be a historian who needed to study the artifact. Maybe if she 'borrowed' it and brought it home to study it more in-depth, she could bring it back a few days later. Sneak it back during the dead of night, maybe with a little 'sorry' sticker on it. That wouldn't be so bad. Would it?

By the time her meal was finished, she still had a couple of hours before the fireworks, so when the server came by to take her empty plate, Cassidy ordered a cup of coffee. Her day was going to be a late one, so it wouldn't hurt to have more caffeine in her system.

CHAPTER SIX

The sky had grown dark, but the city was still alive with celebration. After Cassidy finished her second cup of coffee, she left the pub, which was now almost full of patrons. She wandered around the town for a little while, admiring the architecture while getting an idea of how crowded the streets would be this time of night. Most of the people she saw were heading towards the field, and as she made her way towards the museum, she saw fewer and fewer people around.

Turning onto the pedestrian street where the museum was located, she was pleased to see that there was only one other person in view. They were moving at a quick pace towards the other end of the street, and Cassidy wondered what they could be hurrying towards. There was only the park, forest, and cliffside at that end. Perhaps the fireworks were visible from the cliffside, and the person was hurrying to get a good seat? Whatever it was, at least they'd soon be out of sight and the street empty except for her.

As she walked past the museum, she double-checked that the lights were out and that nobody was inside. That was something she hadn't considered before now, that there might be a security guard on duty, but luckily there was nobody around. She wondered what the crime rates for this area must have been like, for there to be such lax security. Did nobody ever steal anything in this world?

Most of the buildings on the street were pressed up against each other, but because of the museum's older design it had a small alleyway beside it. After making sure that nobody was around to see her, Cassidy slipped into the alley and made her way to the back of the museum. There was a large fence separating this area from the other houses, and when she looked around there were no lights on in any of the windows that she could see. Everyone was probably at the field by now.

Making her way over to the door, she heard the first sounds of fireworks exploding in the air and knew that it was time to get moving. There were two locks on the back door, one on the door handle and one that was a deadbolt. The deadbolt would be more difficult to pick, but it wouldn't be impossible. Luckily, working with Gamgee meant that she could get the best supplies and not have to resort to hairpins.

She quickly opened the lock on the handle, all the while keeping an ear out for anyone who might be close by. There wasn't much light back here, other than the moonlight and occasional glow from the fireworks, but if someone was to stumble through and find her back here, she'd have a heck of a lot of explaining to do. Moving up to the deadbolt, she noticed that it was already unlocked. The employees must have forgotten to lock it, which was lucky for her. This town really was a thief's paradise.

Slowly opening the door, Cassidy tried to stop it from creaking as she slipped into the museum. Closing the door behind her, she noticed that there was also a chain lock hanging lazily next to the door. Shaking her head, she wondered if she should leave a note for the employees to be better about locking up at night. Not that a chain lock would have stopped her, but it would have taken her much longer to break in if she'd had to tangle with a deadbolt and a chain, and too many deterrents could make a person think that something wouldn't be worth the trouble.

With the door closed, there wasn't much light, so she paused to let her eyes adjust to the darkness. She wasn't yet in the museum proper — it was more like an enclosed porch with stairs to her right that led down, and another door on her left.

She cautiously walked forward, stepping lightly on the floor, and tried the handle for the door. The handle turned easily and she almost laughed out loud. Other than the artifact, there wasn't much in this museum worth stealing, but she still thought it'd be harder than this. Maybe they had figured that since there were two more copies of the artifact, they didn't have to put that much effort into protecting this one. And if that were the case, maybe nobody would mind if she happened to borrow it for a few days...

Keeping her mind on the task, she carefully stepped into the museum, waiting to hear if there were any alarms that might alert someone to her presence. During her earlier visit she hadn't seen any motion sensors, alarms, or other security systems, but it was possible that they might be hidden and would set off if anyone came nearby. Luckily, it was silent except for her breathing and the occasional muffled firework. Moving quietly and carefully, she headed straight for the artifact, not paying attention to anything else in the museum. The room with the artifact had two windows facing the street, both tall and rectangular. She paused to look out, but from this distance she could only see an empty street. Some light came in through the windows, but it didn't fall far inside the room, and the centre area where the pedestal was located was far enough away from the light to not be touched by it.

Cassidy crept up to the pedestal, being careful not to get too close because of the rope barrier. When she figured she was near enough, she stood with her back to the window and used her penlight to locate the rope and cautiously step over it. Then she used the concentrated beam of light to look at the bottom of the glass box on the pedestal, shaking her head as she noticed that there was nothing holding it in place. There were no screws or grips, or anything else that might make this job even the slightest bit harder. Maybe they wanted her to get a close up view of this statue. Pocketing the penlight, she put her hands on opposite corners of the glass, being careful not to leave handprints, and lifted it up and over. She placed the glass carefully on the floor and turned back to the artifact.

There was nothing there.

Her body froze, her hands half-way to where the statue had been sitting just hours ago. Taking out her penlight she flashed it over the area where the artifact should have been, but there was nothing but empty space. She wondered if perhaps the statue was some kind of illusion that was only visible inside the box, but that seemed like a lot of effort for a simple museum. Earlier it had looked like a real object, not some kind of trick of the mind, so where was it? Did they lock it up at the end of the day? Was that why the security was such a joke?

Her mind raced. What should she do now? The best action would be to put the glass back on and get the heck out of here. Obviously she'd been outsmarted by the employees, and although she could probably wander through this building to her heart's delight, it would be best to cut her losses and head back through the portal. It was growing late, after all, and the fireworks had died down a few minutes ago.

She bent down to pick up the glass box, but before she could grab hold of it a loud noise startled her. Doors slammed open and light flooded the room, almost blinding her. Cassidy instantly stood up straight as people in dark uniforms raced into the room, surrounding her.

CHAPTER SEVEN

"Stop what you're doing!"

"Put your hands up!"

"Stay where you are!"

The orders came from everywhere as eight people in dark uniforms surrounded her, pointing weapons at her. Cassidy obediently put her hands in the air, her eyes sweeping the bright room as her mind calculated if there was a way out of this. The people surrounding her were all wearing uniforms with badges on them. Had she missed a silent alarm?

"I'm sorry," she said, her eyes still adjusting to the light. "I'll leave right away. I promise."

"You aren't going anywhere," one of them said, in almost perfect English. "You're under arrest for the theft of the Artifact of Harmony."

Cassidy frowned. "Wait. What?"

"You are under arrest for the theft of the Artifact of Harmony," the woman repeated, her voice tinged with impatience. "Please co-operate or we will be forced to—"

"Hold on!" Cassidy interrupted, still holding her hands in the air. "I didn't steal the statue. It was gone when I came in."

The other officers looked confused, but the woman who'd spoken continued her steely gaze. She was older, with grey streaks in her short brown hair, but her body looked broad and strong. Judging by the number of stripes on her uniform, she was a higher rank than the other officers, maybe even the captain.

"It's gone because you stole it," the captain replied, her voice filled with conviction.

"If I stole it, where is it?" Cassidy countered.

"In your backpack."

"Check it."

The captain looked uncertain, but then she turned to a young officer standing next to her and nodded at him. He put his weapon away and walked over to Cassidy, taking hold of her backpack. It was a strange and awkward dance as Cassidy tried to slip out of the backpack while keeping her hands in the air and in plain sight. She hoped that she could put her arms down once she was proven innocent. Television shows always underplayed how exhausting it was to hold your hands in the air for a long period of time.

The officer rummaged through her backpack, and although she couldn't see him, she could hear him making a few curious noises, probably trying to make sense of everything she'd stuffed in there.

While she waited, Cassidy wondered what her next move should be. At first she'd wanted to run out of here, but that was before she'd been accused of a crime she hadn't committed. Sure, stealing the artifact had crossed her mind more than once today, but it had been missing before she'd arrived, and she'd be darned if she was going to be accused of a crime she hadn't committed.

The officer walked over to the captain, holding out the backpack. He sighed and shook his head. "It's not in here, Captain."

"Then she hid it somewhere," the captain replied.

"And then I went back to replace the glass?" Cassidy shook her head. "It'd make more sense to replace it right after taking the statue from the pedestal or to leave it on the floor and get out quickly."

Her words made the captain frown, and she hoped it was because they made sense.

"You talk like a thief," the captain said.

"But on this occasion I'm not. I only wanted a closer look, honest. I wanted to study it. I'm an archeologist."

"You could have applied to the museum for a permit," the man holding her backpack replied.

Cassidy nodded. "I'll be sure to remember that next time."

"No matter what," the captain said, her voice filled with authority. "You have been caught breaking into the museum and an artifact has been discovered missing. You will have to accompany us to the police station for processing."

Cassidy's mind raced as she felt panic creeping up inside of her. She couldn't get arrested. If they put her behind bars, how could she prove that she was innocent? And, more importantly, how long would it take before they figured out that she wasn't from here?

"Look," she said firmly, "I didn't steal the artifact, but I can help you find it. Just give me the chance to clear my name and I'll see to it that you get your artifact back."

"We don't even know your name," the young officer said.

"Cassidy Cane," she replied. "It's a great name, and one I'd hate to see tarnished by false accusations."

The captain shook her head. "Even if I allowed that, there's still the breaking and entering."

"Fair enough. Honestly, I have no qualms about being accused of a crime I committed, but I didn't steal anything. And the longer you fight with me, the more time the actual thief has to get away with your artifact."

The captain paused to think. After a while, the officer on the other side of her whispered, "Are you seriously considering this, Captain?"

"She doesn't have the artifact on her," the captain answered in a low voice. "If she'd stolen it, where is it? Why is she here and not the artifact?"

The other officer tried to think of a reply, but wasn't able to say anything.

"All of you can leave," the captain said. "Jensen, you stay."

The other officers looked confused and surprised, but everyone obeyed the order. Six of the eight officers filed out of the museum, leaving Cassidy, the captain, and the man holding her backpack —whose name was apparently Jensen — behind.

The captain put her weapon away, but she left the holster open so that she could reach it quickly if needed.

"You can put your arms down," the captain said to Cassidy, "but don't try anything funny. We don't like to use weapons, but if I have to take you down, I will."

Cassidy nodded and lowered her arms. Something in the captain's voice told her that the woman wasn't kidding, so she stayed where she was. If she could gain these people's trust, it would be a big step towards clearing her name and getting out of here without going to jail.

Now that the immediate threat of being arrested or shot was gone, Cassidy could focus on the more important subject — where was the artifact and who took it?

"If I might ask a question," Cassidy started carefully, not wanting to step on any toes, "was the artifact definitely on this podium when the museum closed up for the night? Or was it stored in a vault or in another room?"

The captain paused. "I'll have someone contact the employees who closed and check on that."

"Oh, and could you ask them if they'd locked the back entrance?" Cassidy added. "The deadbolt and chain lock were open when I arrived."

The captain gave her a strange look, but then she took out a radio and called her orders back to the station.

Cassidy glanced around the room, trying to see if there were any clues that might prove she wasn't the thief. She didn't see any visible footprints or dirt tracked around the floor, but even if there had been any, the police raid would have made it impossible to tell which tracks belonged to who. Turning to the pedestal, she looked for anything that might have been accidentally dropped on the floor, but all she noticed was some smudging on the glass box. When she'd lifted it she'd only touched the edges, but there was one smudge right in the centre of the glass on the side, and another on the opposite side. Those definitely hadn't been there when she'd visited the museum earlier, and surely one of the employees would have cleaned it off if they'd noticed it after closing. It looked like someone with sweaty palms had lifted the glass. Not exactly a master-stroke of thievery.

While the captain continued talking to the station, Cassidy turned her attention to the young man. He had light brown skin, with brown hair cut regulation short, and his dark eyes regarded her curiously. He had the air of someone who hadn't been in the job for a long time, but definitely wasn't new to it.

"How did you know that I was in here?" Cassidy asked him. "Did I trip some kind of alarm?"

He shook his head. "We had a concerned citizen call us. They said that they'd noticed someone in the museum after hours and wanted the police to take a look."

Cassidy frowned. She'd glanced through one of the windows on her way to the alley and hadn't been able to see much more than shadows inside. She supposed that there was a possibility that someone could have noticed her moving around, but they'd have to have looked in at the right moment or have been watching for a while. Her luck must have been used up during the tournament. Un-less...

"Did the concerned citizen who called you stick around? Did you meet up with them when you got here?"

Jensen shook his head. "There was nobody in the area when we got here, but that's not strange. Most people who call in tips leave before the police arrive."

He had a point, but she was starting to wonder if maybe the call hadn't been from a concerned citizen, but instead from someone hoping to pin a crime they'd committed on someone else. It was a fact that someone had been in the museum before her, and that this person would have a very good reason for calling the police and splitting before they got here. It was far-fetched, but it made more sense than a passerby getting lucky. If the thief noticed her coming in here, then they might have decided to stick around and call the cops once she was inside, framing her for the theft. And if that was the case, then the real thief might not be far away.

"The museum closed at six," she said, mostly speaking to herself. "It started to get dark around nine, and I came in at ten. It'd be risky for someone to break in during daylight, because anyone could see inside and call the cops, so they'd likely waited until after dark..." She paused. "So they may be close by after all..."

The captain finished with her radio, and informed them that the artifact had been left on the pedestal at the end of the day. They'd need to make a couple more calls to confirm about the locks, but that wasn't a priority, as they already knew that someone else had been in here. Cassidy quickly pointed out the marks on the glass, and explained that the real thief might still be close.

"We have to hurry," Cassidy said. "Every second we delay is more time for the thief to get away!"

She could see that the captain wanted to move but was also wrestling with the fact that she'd have to trust a stranger who'd already proven themselves to be untrustworthy.

"How do I know that you won't run away and leave us with nothing? In fact, how do I know that you weren't working with them?"

Cassidy knew she needed to be smart about her answers, and fast. "I'm not working with the thief because you caught me and not them. And if I *had* been working with them, I'd be extremely angry right now because they left me here to take the fall, so I'd want to find them out of pure spite. I have nothing but my word right not, but I know not to run away because you'll hunt me down and you kind of scare me."

For a second it looked like the captain was going to smile, but she quickly masked it. "Jensen, keep an eye on her and don't let her out of your sight for a second. If she somehow manages to find the artifact, call me immediately. You two do your thing, I'll conduct my own search, and hopefully the two will run together at the end."

When Cassidy looked over at Jensen she saw a surprised look on his face, but then his expression neutralized.

"Yes, Captain."

The captain nodded at him. Then she walked over to Cassidy and gave her a stern look, the kind that would turn most people into a quivering mess of fearfulness, before moving towards the pedestal. As she examined the glass box, she noticed that neither Cassidy nor Jensen had moved and turned to them.

"Well, get going already," she said. "I thought time was of the essence."

The two of them quickly obliged and hurried toward the exit.

CHAPTER EIGHT

"Well, where should we go first?" Jensen asked as the two of them stepped outside into the cool night air. He handed over her backpack. "Know of any secret thief hangouts in Vandby? Some kind of illicit black market?"

Cassidy shook her head. "Unfortunately not." She looked around the streets, trying to figure out where the thief might have gone after stealing the artifact. There weren't many people around, but she knew that the next street had some bars along it, and that it was sure to have people around, even with the fireworks. However, at the other end was the park and the forest.

She thought back to the smudged handprints on the glass. The thief been nervous about something, and nervous people usually tried to avoid crowds. If someone noticed that they were sweating or nervous, and asked if they were okay, and then there was a risk that the whole thing would fall apart. The woods were much safer.

Her eyes widened as she remembered the person hurrying towards the park just as she turned onto the street. She'd thought that the person had been running to see the fireworks, but what if it was because they'd just stolen something and were making a quick getaway? Maybe they'd looked back and saw her sneak behind the museum and decided to use that opportunity to call the police. Now that she thought about it, the forest would be a good place to hide out for a few hours or to hide the artifact in. Then the thief could wait until the heat died down and safely take the artifact somewhere else.

"I think we should go to the forest," she said to Jensen. "The city's full of people celebrating Landing Day, but there's probably not a lot of people in the forest."

"Sometimes kids hang out in the woods, but I guess most people would be near the field tonight," Jensen said, uncertainty tinging his voice. She worried that he might disagree, but then he motioned for her to start walking.

They walked in silence, being careful to check every alley they passed, just in case. It gave Cassidy time to wonder just how good of a cop Jensen was. He must be a good one, if the captain decided to let him watch her. Perhaps he was secretly as ruthless as the captain was.

"So, do you get a lot of people trying to steal the artifact?" she asked, in an attempt to make small talk.

He shook his head. "Most people understand that the artifact is very important, not just to this town, but to all the people who live on Vinland. That's why we spoke in English when we burst in, because we knew someone who lived here would never try to steal it."

"But aren't there two other artifacts in different towns? Why make such a fuss about this one?"

"There are, and those have never been stolen either." He gave her a pointed look. "If you'd studied the history of the artifact, you'd know that while it's a very beautiful piece, its importance is symbolic. When the Vikings first landed here, they never would have survived if it hadn't been for the help of the indigenous peoples. Could you imagine what would have happened if they'd decided to treat each other as hostile? How many needless lives would have been lost? These artifacts show that we are stronger together, and are a reminder that it's better to be peaceful and respectful."

"Is there a monetary value to the artifact?"

He shook his head again. "The woods that it's made of could easily be found elsewhere, and there are skilled carvers and artists all over the island that could make something similar, although it'd be a lot newer. Replicas can be bought as souvenirs in all shapes and sizes. In fact, I've got one." Reaching into his pocket, he pulled out a set of keys. After some shuffling, he held up a keychain that was the shape of the artifact but only an inch and a half high.

"Neat," Cassidy said, admiring the replica, but inside she was kicking herself for not looking closer at the souvenir stores. If she'd been smart and purchased a replica then she could have avoided this whole misunderstanding. ...Well... That wasn't entirely true. Most replicas weren't as detailed, so she'd probably still have found herself itching to get a look at the real thing. Perhaps getting caught by the police was an inevitability.

"So the artifact is really important to this town, huh?" she said as they walked.

"To some, yes," he replied. "There are a few superstitions around it, actually. Some say that if an artifact were to ever disappear then a terrible calamity would befall this island and it would be destroyed, sinking below the waves, never to be seen again."

"Wow. If that's the case, you should definitely get better security for it."

He frowned and turned to her, but when he noticed she was trying to make a joke, he relaxed a bit. "I'm sure that we'd be able to remain civilized even if it wasn't here. But I'm sure we'd all rather not test that theory."

Cassidy wanted to say that superstitions usually started somewhere, but figured it'd be better to keep silent.

"So what does a tournament champion want with our artifact anyway?" Jensen said, turning the conversation around to her.

"How did you...?"

"I watched the tournament before my shift started," he explained. "Plus I saw the knife and medal in your backpack when I was searching through it. So, what was your plan? Come here, win the tournament, steal the artifact, and hightail it out of here?"

"I wasn't going to steal it," Cassidy protested. "I wanted a closer look and I didn't know about appealing to the museum, so I made a stupid decision."

"Stupid is right."

"Or," she countered, "was it a great decision, because if I hadn't been there to take the fall, you never would have known about the theft until tomorrow morning, and the thief would probably be in another country by then."

He looked like he wanted to argue with her, but didn't end up saying anything, which she took as a win.

"So, did you always want to be a cop?" she asked.

"Mostly. Did you always want to be a thief — I mean,

an archeologist?"

"Are you making fun of me?" she said, pretending to be aghast.

He smirked. "I can't arrest you yet, so I figured I'd mock you."

"Fair enough." His words reminded her that even if she helped find the artifact, they'd still want to bring her in for breaking into the museum. As soon as the real thief was discovered, she'd have to hightail it out of here.

They stepped out into the park, and after seeing that nobody was in the area, they headed for the forest. Cassidy wondered if the thief would risk taking one of the trails or if they'd be paranoid enough to blaze their own. Probably the latter.

"Look for any newly formed paths," she instructed Jensen. If they ended up not finding anything then they could go down a regular path.

It only took a few minutes before she spied an area with broken branches a few feet from the main trail entrance. Looking at one of the branches she saw that it was a new break. A wide smile broke out on her face. A nervous and paranoid thief was much easier to follow than a sly and logical one.

"This way," she instructed Jensen, and he obediently followed her. It occurred to her that she wasn't explaining her thought process, and that he wasn't asking her to explain. Was he able to pick up on her reasoning or was he simply following her blindly until finally, he'd had enough and felt like arresting her? Maybe if she didn't find the artifact in an hour, he'd knock her over the head and take her to the station. The captain hadn't given them a time limit, but Cassidy had a feeling that they wouldn't want to spend hours or days on this. Hopefully she was on the right path.

Jensen offered her a flashlight to light the way, which she took as a good sign. He might arrest her after all this was over, but at least he was helping her now. Cassidy kept the flashlight focused on the ground, not wanting it to shine through the forest and give anyone notice that they were coming. Unfortunately, she couldn't do much about the branches and leaves that crunched under their feet. Her only comfort was that the thief had left an easy path to follow. As they walked, she continued to spy more broken branches and footsteps, letting those lead her way.

After ten minutes of walking, Cassidy and Jensen passed close to a group of six kids sitting around a lantern in an open area, passing around a bottle. They had been talking and laughing, so hadn't heard their incoming footfalls.

"Hey, you guys seen anyone come through here in the past while?" Cassidy said loudly.

The group startled, looking at her guiltily. Then one of them noticed Jensen.

"Cops! It's the cops!" he yelled, panicking.

"No, it's not," Cassidy said, but the group had already risen to their feet, ready to bolt. The one holding the bottle looked confused, like they were unsure whether to throw it into the woods or run away with it and finish it later.

"Sit back down," Jensen said in a very official-sounding voice, and the kids obeyed, nervously taking their places around the lantern. "Now, if you answer our questions, I'll do my best to forget what you've been doing out here. Okay?"

Cassidy was impressed. Jensen could have a real authority about him when he wanted to. She turned to the kids. "So, have you seen anyone come through here in the past hour?"

The kids stayed silent, but then one of them raised his hand and spoke. "I don't know how long, but a while ago someone came crashing by. They saw us and quickly hurried off. That's it."

"Did they look like they were holding something or had a large bag?"

"Don't know," the same kid said. "It was really dark and they were fast."

Cassidy tried to think of anything else to say, but it was all variations on the same questions. "Well, thanks for that."

"Thank you," Jensen said.

The kids stayed silent and wide-eyed as the two of them made their way back on the trail, watching as they walked away.

"Nice job," Cassidy whispered to Jensen once they were out of ear-shot. "Those kids were terrified. You sure you're not going to report them?"

He shook his head. "Hanging out in the woods is a rite of passage for some kids, and they don't seem to be out of control or doing anything stupid. After this scare, they'll likely call it quits for the night, in case I change my mind."

She turned back to the trail, carefully guiding them further into the woods. She wondered how far the woods went and if they'd have to travel all the way through, eventually ending up on the opposite side of the town. Or would they wind around, back to where they started? It could be easy enough to lose direction without a compass.

Eventually they came to a clearing with a rocky hill on one side. Cassidy looked around for a sign of the trail continuing but there were no more broken branches. There was a well-worn path nearby and she wondered if the thief had gained enough of their nerves back to take it out instead of continuing to plow through the trees.

"Where to now?" Jensen asked.

"Not sure." She paused and looked around the clearing again. The trail had been pretty easy so far, and she'd been hoping the rest of it would be the same. How great would it be to find the thief cowering in fear at the end of the trail, the artifact sitting next to them? But things were never that easy in real life. All she needed to do was figure out which path the thief took and they'd be back in business.

Going up to the trees, she searched for recently broken branches. The clearing wasn't very big, so as soon as she'd ruled out everything else, they could go down the path and continue following the thief. Behind her, Jensen was looking around the clearing, staring at the ground. She was about to ask him to search the trees, but figured that maybe he'd find some footprints that would help them, and let him continue doing his own thing.

As she searched, she thought back to what the kid had said, about how the person had come through the woods a while ago. It had to be their suspect, but how much time had passed since the cops found her in the museum? It wasn't that long, maybe thirty minutes, tops. Was that long enough to count as 'a while?'

She paused. Perhaps the thief hadn't called the cops on her, perhaps it had been a concerned citizen after all.

A startled sound behind her broke her from her thoughts, and when she spun around she saw someone jump from the shadows and lunge for Jensen.

CHAPTER NINE

The stranger crashed into Jensen and the two of them fell to the ground, wrestling with each other.

"Stop it!" Cassidy said, pointing her flashlight at the person, and raising her left arm and holding her fingers like a gun. She hoped that in the darkness he would think she had a weapon and stop, and sure enough, it worked.

"Please don't hurt me!" a low voice said, sitting back and raising his arms in the air.

Jensen pulled himself to his feet and quick pulled his own weapon, training it on the stranger.

"I'm sorry!" the man continued. "I didn't mean to do any of this! I swear!"

"What are you doing here?" Cassidy asked, keeping the light of the flashlight focused on his face. He was blinking and turning his head in an effort to stay out of the bright glow, but she didn't move the light. She didn't understand why he was still here. He should have had plenty of time to hide the statue and get out, but instead he'd chosen to hide.

"I'm waiting for someone," he responded, fear creeping into his voice.

Something in his tone unsettled her and Cassidy quickly glanced behind, searching for a shape in the shadows. She couldn't see anything in the darkness, but moved away from the trees anyway, stepping closer to the stranger while holstering her imaginary weapon.

"Did you steal the Artifact of Harmony?" Jensen asked, getting straight to the point. The man didn't say anything. "We tracked you here, so it'd be best for you to tell us the truth."

The man was breathing heavily and shaking, and Cassidy wondered if Jensen should ask the question again.

"*He* made me do it," the man said, his voice a strangled whisper.

The words sent an unexplained shiver down her back and Cassidy looked at the trees again, shining the flashlight around. She saw nothing, but still felt unnerved. She brought the flashlight back to the stranger, but instead of shining it in his eyes, she held the light in a way that she could see him without blinding him. He had short blond hair and pale skin, and was wearing a black hooded sweater and black pants.

"Who is *He*?" Jensen asked.

"I don't know. He found me on the street earlier today and said he needed to talk to me. Then he started saying all of this stuff about my family and my home and how they'd all be in danger if I didn't do what he asked..."

Cassidy exchanged a look with Jensen, both of them caught off guard by the strange admission.

"Noah?" Jensen said, taking a closer look at the man. "Is that you?"

The stranger paused and looked hard at the two people interrogating him. "Jensen? And who's that?"

"Her name's Cassidy and she's been helping me," Jensen replied. "So you're saying that someone threatened you and made you steal the Artifact of Harmony?"

Noah nodded emphatically. "I didn't want to do it, but he knew my address, and my wallet and keys were missing, so I knew he'd be able to find where I lived. I was supposed to meet him a while ago to give him the statue, but he never showed up. Do you think it's all an elaborate prank or do you think he's on his way to my house?"

It now made sense to Cassidy why it had been so easy to find the thief, because he wasn't a thief — he was some unfortunate local who'd been roped into this.

Jensen put his weapon away and took out his radio, calling the station and asking them to check in on Noah's apartment and family ASAP. "Now, what does this person look like?" Jensen asked.

"I don't know. He was fair skinned and wore a hat, so I couldn't see his eyes. I think his hair might have been auburn, short, mostly hidden under the hat."

"Okay," Jensen said, keeping his voice calm and soothing. "I'm going to take you back to the station so you can tell us everything. Okay?"

Noah nodded.

"But first, where is the artifact?"

Noah took in a deep breath and reluctantly pointed to the large stone he'd been hiding behind. Cassidy kept an eye on him as Jensen walked around the stone and retrieved a black sports bag from the darkness.

"I'm so sorry," Noah said, his voice filled with regret.

"It's okay," Jensen reassured him. He opened up the bag and took out a bulky object wrapped in a thick fabric. Unwrapping it, he saw that it was the artifact. Nodding to himself, he carefully re-wrapped the artifact and put it back in the bag. Then he took out his radio again and called the captain, letting her know that they had found the culprit in the forest and were on their way back to the station with the artifact, and that he'd radio as soon as they were out of the woods.

"Let's get back to town," he said.

Noah's eyes grew wide and he looked at the dark trees surrounding them. "But... What if *He's* out there?"

"We could take the trail," Cassidy said. "It would be harder for someone to sneak up on us." She didn't know if it was the power of suggestion, but knowing that the person who'd threatened Noah was still out there made her feel uneasy. He could be in the woods, watching them, right now. Taking the trail would be safer than trying to go back through the path that had led them here. Although it wasn't very wide, it left more space around them and would give them a clear path to run down if they heard anyone approaching.

"I agree," Jensen nodded. "I'll take the lead, Noah will follow, and you bring up the end. Keep an eye out, and if we hear or see anything suspicious we stop and group up."

They began walking along the trail, taking a quick pace. Jensen held his flashlight and the bag with the artifact. Cassidy had offered to hold the bag for him, but he'd quickly declined. She didn't take it personally, considering how she'd been caught breaking into the museum. She obediently took up the rear, sandwiching Noah in between them, in the safest place. She'd dug into her backpack to find her own flashlight — the penlight wouldn't be much help out here — and was using it to shine around the forest, looking for anyone who might be following them. She didn't see anything, and for a moment she wondered if Noah's paranoia had transferred to her, but it was better to be safe than sorry. She tried to keep an ear out for any strange noises, but it was difficult to hear anything over the sound of their own footfalls. Despite their path being a well-worn trail, it was still covered with broken branches and dried leaves. At least they didn't have to dodge tree branches and large roots.

Noah seemed to grow more and more nervous the further they walked. His head darted to the sides, as if on a swivel. Cassidy thought he'd get calmer the closer they got to town, but that wasn't the case. This mysterious man had really done a number on him.

"Shouldn't be long now," Jensen said quietly, and Cassidy wondered if he was saying this to try and calm Noah. She had no idea where they were or how close they were to town, but she hoped that Jensen's words were correct. The sooner Noah got put into police custody, the better.

It occurred to her that she'd also get put into police custody once they made it out of the forest. Her original plan had been to sneak away once the artifact had been found, but now that there was a possible supervillain stalking them through the woods she didn't feel like doing that. Maybe she didn't have to run away. Maybe they'd take it easy on her since she'd successfully discovered the artifact. Noah's story concluded that she hadn't been involved in the plan, so maybe they'd give her a slap on the wrist and let her go. After all, without her help the artifact would probably have been half-way to Russia by now. If Russia even existed in this world...

A loud noise broke her concentration and drew her attention to her right, where it sounded as if someone had stepped on and broken a large branch.

Noah let out a shriek. "He's here! He's coming for me!" He pushed past Jensen, shoving him to the side, and raced down the dark trail. Sensing that this was her moment to flee, Cassidy started to run after him, but then she noticed that Jensen wasn't getting up. She shone her flashlight around the woods, but there was no movement or any more noises, other than Noah's footsteps quickly fading away. She told herself that she was being paranoid, and quickly moved over to Jensen.

He was breathing, but unconscious. She figured that he must have hit his head when Noah had shoved him. Cassidy sized up the situation she was in. She really wanted to get out of the forest, but that would involve carrying Jensen, the artifact, and a flashlight. If anyone was watching them, she'd be a very easy target. But she couldn't stay here, and every time she thought about leaving Jensen behind she felt terrible.

Sighing, she shouldered the bag with the artifact, being careful not to knock it against her backpack, and lifted Jensen to his feet, placing his arm across her shoulders. Her muscles still ached from her earlier activities in the competition, but luckily Jensen wasn't much bigger than she was, and she managed to keep him upright. Holding him by the waist with her left arm, she held the flashlight in her other hand and shone it along the path.

"I hope you were right about us almost being out," she whispered to his unconscious form. She could almost feel unseen eyes watching her, following her through the forest, and had to resist shuddering. Taking in a deep breath, she told herself that there was nothing to be afraid of.

Her progress was slow, and she stopped often to make sure that there were no sounds of someone following her. She was glad she'd had a rest after the tournament, as dragging another human was not the easiest activity. Jensen didn't wake up, but every so often he'd let out a groan, and she was thankful that his injury didn't seem to be too terrible.

Finally she saw a light and realized that the path was coming to an end. Breathing a sigh of relief, she sped up, hurrying towards the park.

Once she was out in the open, all of her fears went away. She wondered if she'd overreacted. She was old enough not to get scared by tales of boogeymen, but there was something about Noah's tale and being in a dark, unfamiliar forest that had brought out long-forgotten fears. Whatever it was, she didn't want to go back in that forest any time soon.

It was late and there was nobody else in sight, not even Noah, so she dragged Jensen's body over to the nearest bench and sat him down. Opening up the bag, she carefully unwrapped the artifact, telling herself that she was doing it to make sure it hadn't been damaged in the fall. It was so beautiful and complex, and again she felt the call to take it with her. It would so easy to grab it and run to the cliffside, escaping back into her own world. Jensen was knocked out, but he knew that she was innocent. And he'd never know if she had taken it or if it had been lost in the woods during his fall. It would be so easy.

But as she stared at the artifact she couldn't help remembering all of Jensen's words about what the artifact represented. If she took this statue through the portal would she bring about a curse and sink this island?

Why would the universe present her with this kind of opportunity if it didn't want her to take the artifact?

Sighing, she looked from the statue to Jensen, very aware that time was ticking away.

CHAPTER TEN

When Jensen awoke, his head was pounding and someone was calling his name. Opening his eyes, he saw Captain Andersen standing in front of him. It was still dark outside, but there was enough light around to see the concerned look on her face.

"Where is she?" she asked.

It took a few seconds for him to realize who she was talking about. He looked around, noticing that he was in the park outside the forest. There were a couple officers standing further away and a few onlookers, but Cassidy was nowhere in sight. His eyes widened and he searched more frantically before his gaze fell on the black bag at his side. Opening it up, he lifted out the bundle and quickly unwrapped it, revealing the artifact.

Sighing, he leaned back on the bench. "I guess she's gone," he replied.

Andersen looked at the artifact. "At least she got it back for us before clearing off. I half-expected that she'd run off with it when I got here and saw only you."

"But why are you here? I thought you were waiting for us at the station?"

"Got a call from her on your radio. Said to come here because you'd been injured in the woods."

Recalling the last memory he had before waking up, Jensen looked around again. "We need to find Noah Leth. He got scared and ran away. He's been mixed up in this whole thing and we need to keep him safe."

Andersen gave a half-smile. "He's already at the station. Raced in, looking like he'd run a marathon, apologizing all over the place. When I left, Ostergard was still trying to calm him down."

"Then I guess this case is over..." Jensen said, but he couldn't help looking around the clearing again. It seemed fitting that Cassidy had disappeared like a ghost in the night, but he would have at least liked to say goodbye. As well as thank you. If it hadn't been for her, they might never have gotten the artifact back.

"Don't look so lost," Andersen said. "At least she saved me the trouble of having to figure out whether to arrest her or let her go."

Jensen laughed. That she had.

"Now, let's get you to the hospital to get checked out."

***

From where she was watching, Cassidy saw the whole interaction between the captain and Jensen. She couldn't hear anything, but neither of them looked furious or upset, so she considered herself to be safe. After calling the station to have someone check on Jensen, she'd thought about going back to her world, but she didn't want to risk someone stealing the artifact while Jensen was still unconscious. As much as she didn't like the idea, she knew that it'd be best to hide in the forest, so she'd concealed herself in the trees, hoping that there were no supervillains hiding nearby.

It was past midnight when the park was finally empty of onlookers and police. Freeing herself from the forest, she used the moonlight to guide her to the cliff. As she reached the edge, she looked back at the town and wondered if she'd ever be back here. Maybe it'd be best if she stayed away for a while. Maybe the police would spend the rest of their lives talking about the mysterious stranger who'd helped find a stolen artifact. Or maybe she'd be forgotten after a few months.

She thought about the knife she'd won in the competition, and was glad that she was leaving with some kind of artifact to bring back to the professor. A smile broke out over her face and she reached into her pocket, taking out the keychain she'd 'borrowed' from Jensen. The tiny replica wasn't as magnificent as the original, but it would do. Hopefully Jensen would forgive her taking it, considering how she'd left him the real one.

Laughing to herself, Cassidy put some chalk on her hands and started the climb down the cliff, towards home.

ACKNOWLEDGEMENTS

The authors would like to pay special thanks to the *Slipstreamers* committee at Engen Books, including Amanda Labonté, Matthew LeDrew, AJ Ryan, Ellen Curtis, Erin Vance, and, Lauralana Dunne.

Without their tireless efforts, none of this would have been possible.

Special thanks to this episode's editor, AJ Ryan.

COMING SOON!
BOULDERS OVER THE BERMUDA TRIANGLE
BY JD RYOT & PETER FOOTE!

The next incredible episode of Slipstreamers, Boulders Over the Bermuda Triangle, will be available soon, written with Peter J Foote!

When Cassidy enters a portal hovering over the fabled Bermuda Triangle, she finds herself on the strange alien world of Xik'en, located in the hub of an asteroid mine and where lizard-people reign supreme!

What lies hidden below the station, in the Xik'en prison?

SPECIAL BONUS PREVIEW!

We're pleased to present a preview of the first novel by this episode's co-author, Ali House.

The Six Elemental is a 2016 novel, and the first in the Segment Delta Archives series.

The myth of the Six-Elemental is almost seven hundred years old, and the possibility of someone having the power of more than one Element has been thoroughly disproven by science. None of this matters, however, when Kit Tyler receives the power of all six Elements on her twenty-first birthday.

Unsure of how the world will react, or how to wield her powers, Kit keeps this information a secret, swearing that she will reveal it when she is stronger and more worthy. After all, the only thing worse than being a walking myth is being a disappointing one. When the opportunity comes along to help prevent an impending war, she sees this as her chance to prove herself.If she can do this then nobody will question why she, of all people, was chosen.

CHAPTER ONE

Today was Kit Tyler's birthday and there were only two more hours before the damn thing was over with. A person's 21st birthday should be a time of anticipation and celebration, but all Kit could feel was anxiety.

Had her father still been alive, he would have told her what to expect. They would have discussed the pros and cons of Acceptance and, even though the choice was hers, he would encourage her to Accept her element. He would tell her that each and every element had its advantages, and that she shouldn't Deny just because it wasn't the element she wanted. He would say this, but she knew that secretly he'd be hoping she'd receive the element of Electricity, just like him.

Her father would also tell her that everything would be all right if she did not receive a vision. Not receiving a vision didn't mean that there was something wrong with you, it just meant that life had something else in store for you.

But her father's death had deprived her of his company, and she now had to face this day alone. Her mother had changed after her father's death and married a man who was a member of the Church of Humanity – a religious sect which believed that everyone who Accepted an element should burn in hell. Humanists believed that everyone should live like the humans of old – the quote-unquote chosen ones – and deny that which made them unnatural. Kit did not share his opinions in the slightest, which created a rather large rift between her step-father and her, and subsequently her mother and her.

This rift was the reason she had chosen to study on the island of Aesira instead of Briton. Briton had the highest concentration of Humanists in all of Segment Delta, while the people of Aesira mostly followed the Church of Peace. The two islands were connected by an overseas highway, but Aesira might as well have been on the other side of New Earth.

After graduation, she planned on moving even further away, but first she had to get through this day. Kit had spent a long time thinking about this decision, and she still didn't know what to do. Should she honor her father's memory and Accept or should she try to please her mother and step-father and Deny?

Maybe she wouldn't have to make a choice. With less than two hours to go, it appeared that the decision had been made for her. Kit couldn't help but feel disappointed by her lack of a vision. There were a decent number of neutral people in Segment Delta, but most of them were Humanists and made the choice to Deny their element. Very few people were vision-less. It was a one in one thousand chance – lucky her.

As hard as it was to decide, she wanted the choice. Even if she made the wrong decision, at least she'd have had some say in the matter.

She hadn't told many people about today being her birthday. Her roommate, Anya, knew, but Anya also knew about Kit's complicated family relationship. When Kit said that she'd rather spend today alone, Anya agreed not to interfere. They weren't the best of friends, but the two of them had an understanding.

Kit had spent most of the day in her room, alone. She'd paced up and down the room about a hundred times, waiting for her vision. She had no idea when it was going to happen, but she wanted to be prepared, and she definitely didn't want to be around other people.

As the day dragged on without anything happening Kit became more and more anxious. She hadn't left the room for lunch because she didn't want to have her vision in the middle of the lunchroom, but by suppertime she was so hungry that she had to leave her room. As she walked to the lunchroom she couldn't help noticing that every step she took was another second of the day gone – gone without anything happening.

After supper she decided to go to the library and wait out the day there. She gathered an armful of books and hid in the back corner, keeping to herself. At first she was able to concentrate on her reading, but then she noticed how much time had passed. The day was almost over and still she hadn't had a vision. Anxiety was replaced with disappointment. If she was going to get a vision, then surely she'd have had it by now.

Kit tried to concentrate on the book in front of her, but it was impossible. She couldn't help imagining the satisfied smirk that would be on her step-father's face when she told them that she was neutral. Briefly, she considered lying to her family and telling them that she'd Denied, but then she realized that she'd rather be neutral than pretend to be even the slightest bit Humanist.

Checking her watch, she saw that it was almost eleven o'clock. If she stayed in the library until midnight then Anya would be asleep by the time she made it back to the dorm, and if Anya was asleep then she wouldn't have to answer any vision-related questions. Kit sighed and stood up. She was going to need a more interesting book.

She was browsing the mythology section for a book on Ancient Earth deities when suddenly everything went black. A vision of lightening striking the ground with enough force to displace the earth flashed before her eyes, followed by images of a tornado tearing through a forest, a fireball smashing into the side of a mountain, the earth shaking and ripping open, hail the size of golf balls slashing through the air, and a torrent of water flooding through a crevasse. The visions repeated faster and faster until finally she passed out.

$$\text{⚡} \approx \triangle \square \bigcirc \text{✳}$$

It was dark. Faint images of lightening, fire, water, air, earth and ice appeared and disappeared. Kit didn't know what was going on. She'd never heard of someone having six visions before. Was she being given a choice? Could she pick and choose from the six elements? She tried concentrating on Electricity, but the rest of the images wouldn't go away. What did it mean? Was she being offered the choice of all six elements? The images became clearer and she knew that it was true.

But it was impossible. Nobody could have all six elements. She'd been waiting for one vision, not six – she wasn't prepared for this. She had to make a choice. But did she really have a choice? Could she actually Deny something like this? All six elements...

Kit watched as the visions became sharper and more detailed. The raw power of each element fascinated her.

She knew her answer.

$$\text{↯} \approx \triangle \ \square \ \bigcirc \ \text{✳}$$

When Kit regained consciousness, she became aware that there were people staring at her. From the looks of her surroundings she was lying on the floor in the mythology section.

"Are you okay?"

Kit looked to her left, where a concerned woman was kneeling beside her.

"Um, yeah. I think I'm fine," Kit replied. Why were all these people here? "What happened?"

"I don't know. I just heard a scream and came back here. You were lying on the floor, unconscious."

"It must have been..." Kit stopped. "I... I thought I saw something. But I'm fine now. My bad."

Someone helped her to her feet and Kit realized that she was able to stand on her own. She thanked everyone for their concern and exited the library as quickly as possible.

As she walked to her dorm room, she tried not to make eye contact with the few people she passed. She was embarrassed beyond belief. Fainting in public? Screaming in the library? So much for not calling attention to herself...

What about her visions? Was she delusional or had

she actually Accepted all six elements? Science had proven that it was impossible for someone to have more than one element, and who was she to go disproving science? It was more likely that she was neutral and imagined the whole thing?

A tingling feeling on her left wrist told her otherwise. She looked down and saw two blue wavy lines on her wrist, where before there had been only skin. She grabbed her wrist to hide the mark, but that same feeling was suddenly on her right upper arm, then her lower back, then her left ankle, her stomach and her left shoulder-blade. Kit picked up the pace. She had forgotten about the Tattoos – the marks that appeared after Acceptance as proof of your element. She had to get back to her room before anyone noticed.

When she reached her dorm she was relieved to find Anya asleep. The night-light was plugged in – their usual courtesy when one of them went to sleep before the other was back – and in the dim light Kit made her way over to the mirror and looked at herself. Outwardly she hadn't changed much, except for the blue marks of Air on her wrist. On her right arm was a crooked yellow line – Electricity. The green circle on her ankle was for Water, and the three white lines forming a snowflake on her stomach were for Ice. She pulled her shirt off and looked over her shoulder, confirming the brown square for Earth on her lower back and the red triangle for Fire on her left shoulder-blade.

She had six Tattoos. She had six elements. How?

Nobody had ever received more than one element – ever. Well, there was the story about the Six-Elemental, but that was a fairy tale, and it was also almost seven hundred years old. If it was possible to receive all six elements, then surely someone other than her would have done it by now.

So why her? Why now? She was just some girl from Briton. She wasn't in the Forces or working for the ISS. She was an architecture student who didn't even have a job lined up after graduation. Why hadn't this happened to someone more important? Why her?

Should she tell anyone? Something like this didn't happen every day. In fact, it had never happened before – ever! People would treat her like some kind of impossible thing. Would they want to study her? Would she spend the rest of her life in a lab? Maybe they'd want her to join the Forces or work for the ISS. Maybe they'd want her to turn into some kind of super-soldier.

Kit didn't want any of that. She'd taken a few self-defense courses in school, but she wasn't a soldier and had no desire to be one. If the Forces discovered her powers, would they give her a decision or would they make her join them?

And she hadn't even taken into consideration the Followers of Six...

She didn't want to be treated like she was different, or isolated and studied. All she wanted was to live her life the way she wanted.

So she'd have to lie. She'd also have to cover up her Tattoos and keep them covered at all times. Kit swore under her breath. Covering up one would have been annoying enough, but six? She couldn't pretend that they were fakes. It was illegal for tattoo artists to fake a Tattoo, and the punishment wasn't worth the crime, so no one ever broke that law. These Tattoos never faded and never went away, so she'd have to hide them. Forever.

A small part of her wished that she'd Denied. She wasn't the right person for something like this. Why hadn't someone else been chosen instead of her?

Sitting on her bed, Kit put her head in her hands and took a deep breath. She needed to calm down and think of a plan. As long as she had a plan it would all work out, and everything would be fine.

⚡ ≈ △ □ ○ ✳

The next day she 'confessed' to Anya that she was an Electricity Elemental, but instructed her roommate not to tell anyone else because she didn't want word to somehow get back to her family. Electricity was the easiest element to go with, as it was the easiest Tattoo to show off, and it meant that Kit could wear sleeveless or short-sleeved shirts around the room. Anya gave Kit a conspiratorial wink and promised that she would say nothing.

It was getting close to finals, so there was lots of study-ing to do and not a lot of time left for other distractions. There was also the matter of trying to find a job in her field. Any spare time she had went to researching compa-nies, sending out resumes, and traveling to other islands for interviews. It kept her busy, and distractions were more than welcome. When she finally found a job, she was elated.

First, however, she had to get through her finals, which were easy enough considering how much studying she'd put in, and then through the summer – which would be much more difficult. Her mother acknowledged that she was busy and understood that Kit couldn't call them very often, but she was expecting Kit to come back to Briton for a visit after graduation.

Of the six islands in Segment Delta, Briton was the second last island Kit wanted to be on. The last island was Tecken, whose residents had been brainwashed by a megalomaniac and which was now cut off from the rest of the Segment – but it wasn't losing to Briton by much.

Living in Briton had been okay when her father was alive, but her step-father had moved them to a Humanist neighborhood. Kit couldn't understand why someone would want to hate another person for having a power that was built into their EDNA – their very being. So what if their existence was a result of genetic manipulation? They existed. They had thoughts and feelings. And what was so wrong with having purple hair or orange eyes anyway?

Kit's eyes were blue, which was acceptable by Humanist standards, but her hair was the same bright blue that her father's had been. Her step-father had tried to get her to dye her hair a human colour, but Kit always refused. It was only one of the many reasons why she never got along with her step-father – because she constantly reminded him of something he hated.

When she was feeling really indignant, she would think about how all the humans had died, and how they were all that was left. If the humans had been the better species, why weren't they here now? Kit had never dared voice this thought to her step-father, but it was always in the back of her mind whenever he started off on one of his rants.

After graduation, Kit packed all of her belongings into her El-car and reluctantly headed to Briton. On the drive, Kit wondered if she'd be able to cut her visit short. Her new job didn't start for two months and she would save money staying at her mother's house, but eight weeks was a long time to be in Briton. Maybe she could leave after a month. Surely she could last four weeks.

As she stood outside the house, her left hand tugged on the right sleeve of her yellow t-shirt. The sleeve covered her Electricity Tattoo, but not by much. She should have worn a different shirt, but it was too warm for long sleeves. If she walked into the house covered from head to toe, her step-father would know for sure that something was up.

She'd seen a few Humanists who'd converted after Acceptance. They swore to never use their elemental power again, and then they were tattooed with a big black 'X' over their elemental Tattoo. It was a jarring sight to see – which was probably the statement the Humanists were going for. Kit quite liked to look at the yellow lightning bolt on her arm. It reminded her of when she was younger and would ask her father to show her his Tattoo, and he would obediently roll up his pants leg to show her the mark on his ankle. It made her feel closer to him.

It would have been convenient if that Tattoo had been somewhere easier to conceal, like the others, but at least it wasn't on her face or somewhere else that was completely obvious. Apparently there were still miracles in the world.

⚡ ≈ △ ▢ ○ ✳

When she entered the house, Jill and Mich were the first faces Kit saw. Breaking into a smile, Kit dropped her purse on the floor and braced herself for Mich's attack hug. Two seconds later, her half-sister propelled herself into Kit's arms, almost knocking the both of them over.

The two of them were the reason Kit kept coming back to the house. Despite sharing genetics with their father, Kit knew that they didn't share all of his ideals.

"You're back! You're back! You're back!" Mich chanted, jumping up and down with the energy only a seven year old could have.

"Nice hair," Kit teased, making sure that her sleeve was pulled down before righting herself.

Mich, short for Michelle, subconsciously tugged on a loose strand. Mich's hair was naturally a deep green, but it was constantly being dyed black by her father. Right now there was almost an inch of green showing.

"Don't tell Dad," Mich whispered to her, conspiratorially. "I'm waiting to see how long it takes him to notice."

This little rebellion brought a smile to Kit's face.

"Hey, Kit," Jill said from her chair in the living room. She hadn't bothered to get up or take her nose out of her book, but Kit didn't take it personally. Jill was only one year older than Mich, but liked to act five years cooler.

"Good book?"

"The best."

"Where's everyone else?"

"Getting food."

"Glad to see you're working on your vocabulary," she teased.

Jill finally looked up from her book and stuck out her tongue. "I save my vocabulary for important people."

For the next hour, Kit caught up with her half-sisters. It was a good start to the month. She hoped that the rest of it would be just as pleasant, although she seriously doubted it.

When her mother and step-father arrived home, her step-father was first through the door. He looked at her for a few seconds before nodding and walking on. Apparently Kit had passed the first test. Her mother walked in next, her arms full of take-out containers.

"Katherine!" her mother greeted. "How was the drive over?"

"Good. The weather was great."

"I'm so glad to hear. We decided to get take-out for dinner. I'd wanted to go to Zelia's, since I know it was one of your favorites, but it turns out they closed down a few months ago, so we went to Joe's Kitchen instead. Michelle and Jill like the food there."

Mich leaned in close to Kit and whispered, "Don't eat the soup. They hide disgusting vegetables in there."

Kit stifled a laugh. "Let me help you with those, Mom." She walked over and took a few of the containers. The news that Zelia's had closed down wasn't surprising. Over the past year most of her favorite places to eat had closed down and were replaced by more 'traditional' Humanist restaurants. It was yet another sign of the changes happening throughout Briton.

"Wash up, you two," her mother called to Mich and Jill on her way into the kitchen. "Dinner's in ten."

As Kit helped her mother sort through the containers,

she noticed that her step-father was nowhere in sight. She would have liked for him to help out, but she preferred his absence more.

"I've got a couple different salads and sandwiches," her mother said. "They've started growing zucchinis in the south garden, so I've got a salad with that. Well, that's what they're calling them. I'm not sure how it'll taste, but we might as well find out if it's any good."

"I'm sure it'll be fine," Kit replied.

"I see you're wearing those bracelets again."

Kit looked down at the black cuffs that she was wearing around each wrist. After her father's death she'd worn them every day for three years before reluctantly agreeing to take them off. Since her birthday, she realized that they were perfect for covering up her Air Tattoo, and if anybody asked why she could always get sentimental.

"It seemed like a good time to start again," Kit said.

Her mother stopped unpacking and looked at her. "How was your birthday?" she asked, her voice low and serious. "Really?"

Kit paused. After her birthday, she'd told her mother that she was neutral and that she didn't want to discuss it any further. Did her mother suspect her of lying?

"I don't want to talk about it," Kit said, putting as much disappointment into her voice as possible.

"I see." Her mother gave her a half-smile. "Well, you may look like your father, but I guess there's a bit of me in your DNA."

Kit opened her mouth to correct her mother, but then thought better of it.

"I know you wanted to be like him, Katherine, but this

is for the best. Trust me. Now, let's get everything on the table."

As they set the table for dinner, Kit remained silent. How was it best for her to be neutral? The best thing would to be for her to say what she was and for her family to stand by her, but her family couldn't do that. They cared more about some stupid religion than their own daughter.

She felt her hands tightening around the cutlery she was holding, so she paused and collected herself. There was no way she'd make it through the next two months if she couldn't keep her temper in check.

Throughout dinner, her mother talked about Jill and Michelle, telling Kit about their schooling and their summer programs. Kit said very little and her step-father even less. Eventually, though, her mother ran out of things to say and the conversation turned to Kit.

"So, you've got a new job starting in August?" her mother said.

"Yeah. I'm really excited. It's a great company."

"Is it back in Aesira?"

Kit considered her options and decided to go with the truth. "It's in Stanton."

Her mother's eyes widened. "That's... so far away," she said, recovering from the shock. "It's too bad that you didn't get a job in Briton. It'd be nice to have you close."

"I couldn't find a job in Briton," Kit replied. Truthfully, she hadn't even bothered looking.

Her step-father cleared his throat. "I've heard that people are moving out of Stanton. Don't think it's safe being so close to Tecken."

"Two families just moved here from Stanton," her mother confirmed. "And three others in the past two months."

"I'm sure it's fine," Kit said, trying to keep her tone light. "Stanton's leader would warn everyone if it wasn't safe."

"Stanton's gone soft," her step-father continued. "Need more discipline over there."

Kit swallowed hard. Why couldn't they just talk about the weather?

"Papers say that a second invasion is imminent. Erikson's not satisfied with only one island."

"The Briton Truth?" Kit scoffed. If that was her step-father's source, then she had nothing to worry about. The local paper absolutely loved lies, especially when they put Elementals in a bad light.

He turned to her. "They've got people in Stanton. They say that the Elementals are all siding with Erikson. Humanists shouldn't bother going there."

"Good," she muttered under her breath.

"What was that?" he asked, his voice rising.

"It's not true. I spent a weekend in Stanton during my interview. It's perfectly fine."

"That's what they want you to think. Of course, you're more likely to side with Erikson than the rest of us."

Kit felt herself grow strangely still. "Did you just accuse me of being a Tecken supporter?"

"You support Elementals and they're nothing but a bunch of degenerates," he replied, turning back to his supper. "Unless you straighten up and fly right, it's the next logical step."

The table was silent. Kit pressed her lips together to stop the flow of words that wanted to break forth. How her mother could love a man who was so misguided, she would never be able to understand.

He had never been warm to her, but most of his complaints were small. He wanted her to go to church more or stop defending Elementals. Never before had he accused her of something so awful. A Tecken supporter? How could he think for one second that she would ever support a war-mongering megalomaniac? How dare he!?

Pushing her chair back from the table, Kit stood up and turned to leave.

"Where are you going?" her step-father asked.

Kit stayed silent. Her teeth were clenched so hard that her jaw hurt. She was almost out of the room when she felt his hand on her shoulder, turning her to face him.

"I didn't say you could leave," he said.

"If you didn't want me to leave, then you shouldn't have said anything at all," she replied, shaking his hand off her shoulder.

"I'll say what I want in my own home. You're the one bringing in dangerous ideas."

Kit couldn't believe him. "It's not dangerous to think that Elementals deserve to have the power that their EDNA offers them."

"Elementals are a danger to society. No person should have that kind of power. That power is why Tecken was able to invade."

"The first invasion was not the fault of Elementals!" Kit was using all of her restraint not to yell. "Elementals fought against Erikson! There are whole divisions in the

Forces devoted to Elementals!"

"Propaganda," her step-father grumbled.

"As if everything you say hasn't been twisted into some kind of horrible lie just to serve your own selfish needs!" she shot back.

He shook his head. "I used to think that there was hope for you, Katherine. I thought that you being neutral would make you wake up and realize that Elementals are wrong, but you're a lost cause. Nothing good can come from Acceptance."

"Nothing good can come from your mouth."

His arm pulled back and she flinched, but he didn't hit her. Kit saw her mother's eyes widen as her hands flew to her mouth. Jill and Mich were both watching with wide eyes, forks still half-raised.

"This is my house and you will respect me when you are inside it."

She shook her head. "I will respect you when you deserve that respect. For now, I'll settle for tolerating you." She turned away again, but he grabbed her right arm to stop her. She pulled her arm away sharply, breaking his grip, and stepped into the living room. If this was an indication of what the next month would be like, then it would be best for her to avoid her step-father at all times.

"What did you do?" His voice was no longer angry. It had an emptiness that scared her more than his anger ever could.

"What?" She was confused. What had changed?

He grabbed her right arm and pulled her sleeve up to reveal the bright yellow mark on her forearm. "I should have known."

Her mother gasped.

"Of course you're moving to Stanton," he continued. "You'll help Erikson kill every Humanist in the Segment."

Kit clenched her fists. Anger coursed through her body, but this time she didn't try to stop it. She could feel the electricity crackling around her fists.

Fear crossed her step-father's face as he watched her eyes glow yellow, and he took a step back before regaining his composure. "Get the hell out of my house. Get your things and get out and never come back."

As much as she wanted to hit him, she kept her arms still and pulled the electricity back in. Punching him would only prove that all Elementals are violent and she didn't want him to be right about anything.

"Get out now!" he yelled. "If you're not out of here in ten seconds, then I am calling the police and having you arrested!"

She hated herself for giving in to his threat, but she turned away. Her purse was still by the door, so she grabbed it on her way out, heading straight for her El-car. There were certain cops on Briton that would arrest Elementals even if they hadn't done anything wrong, and she was sure her step-father would be able to spin a tale that would get her held in a cell for weeks or even months.

Besides, the sooner she was out of this awful place, the better.

ABOUT THE AUTHOR

Alison House is an Award-Winning, Bestselling author, a Newfoundlander, a playwright, a traveler, and a reader.

House is a graduate of the Fine Arts program at Sir Wilfred Grenfell College and currently resides in Halifax, Nova Scotia, where she works in arts administration and spends more time than a person should in and around theaters.

She has been featured in every open-call collection frm Engen Books. Her first short fiction collection, *The Lightbulb Forest*, was released in February 2020. Her novels include *The Six Elemental* and *The Fifth Queen*.

JD Ryot is the reclusive creator of the *Slipstreamers* series from Engen Books. JD is an avid fan of young adult literature and adventure serials. When asked if they had come to this world through a portal themselves, JD Ryot refused to answer. No record of their birth has ever been found... on this world.